The Land as Viewed from the Sea

The Land as Viewed from the Sea

RICHARD COLLINS

seren

Seren is the book imprint of
Poetry Wales Press Ltd
Nolton Street, Bridgend, CF31 3BN, Wales
www.seren-books.com

ISBN 1-85411-367-4

A CIP record for this title is available from
the British Library

The publisher works with the financial assistance of the
Welsh Books Council.

Printed in Garamond by CPD (Wales), Ebbw Vale.

The Land as Viewed from the Sea

The sea is a great expanse of grey-green and blue cold water, stretching under an opaque winter sky. Across the surface runs a swell; large rollers generated by the wind of a few days ago, continuing their motion from the west until they come up against the land. There the line of waves changes, refracting around headlands and bending to take on something of the shape of the shoreline. The waves, as they approach the shore, are large and smoothly rounded like whale-backs. Their glossy surface is pock-marked by small rain. Around this bay they break onto beaches of sand and shingle, against cliffs and rocky outcrops, and onto man-made harbour walls, breakwaters and embankments. Here they are meeting a shingle beach, each wave hitting with some force, then dissipating among the stones with a rattle and a sigh. The sound is rhythmic and might be soothing. The air is still but the waves have travelled from far away, where there was once a wind. Now, with the momentum of past events, they move steadily onto the shore.

From the beach it is possible to see the whole long curve of the bay stretching away in either direction. To the south, headlands are visible in the distance, the further ones fading and insubstantial like clouds sitting on the horizon. To the north there are mountains close to the coast and a long peninsula, its hilltops visible above the horizon, like a series of islands. In fact the last seeming-island is an island for real, sometimes the beam of its lighthouse can be seen in the night across the bay. Above the beach, at the foot of a small valley that runs down to the sea, is a large mostly empty building, the old stable block for the grand house that once stood close by. It is now used for the storage of farm implements except for the flat upstairs above the stables. The building faces south, looking over the stream, to the other side of the valley. Only a small window on its gable end looks out towards the sea. There are no other houses around and it is a bleak lonely place, cold and exposed, with none of the softening influence of the trees that grow further inland.

In the flat are two people, a man and a woman. During the course of this winter afternoon his words have disturbed her and an argument has ensued. Reason has given way to anger and he has taken to pacing up and down the large room between the clutter of her artists' materials and photographs. Now he stops and looks out of the gable window at the sea. He can't hear its noise as the window is shut against the cold. He is trying to regain calm, to avoid crisis. He turns to her again and sees that her anger is still building as she watches him. But he cannot resist the temptation of saying things that will hurt her – a sentence that includes the word 'hate'. For a moment she is rigid with self-control. She pushes her hair back away from her face. He turns and looks away as she moves towards him. Then there is a sudden movement and he feels her fist hard on his cheek close to his left eye. Sharp bone-against-bone pain.

He moves around her very fast and very carefully. He picks up a half-empty coffee cup and throws it with extraordinary force at the opposite wall, where it shatters, a stain of coffee up to the ceiling and shards flung to each side of the room. Her eyes are round with bewilderment as she looks at the man standing shaking in front of her. It happened very fast. He diverted his anger around her with care and grace as if protecting her from some external harm and she is reminded of protective tendernesses of the past. For a moment they are still. Then she takes his hands and rests herself lightly, cautiously against him.

Then they are on the floor, some clothes discarded, moving hard against each other. More quickly than ever before, they reach the state when, for both of them, the only conscious sense is that of physical pleasure. No thoughts. No self-awareness. No knowledge of the involuntary sounds they make. This for some time. Only later do they regain some sort of consciousness and find themselves in the corner of the room, sweating, tear-stained, and bruised. Breathing hard amid a chaos of fallen books, photographs, and the shards of a coffee cup.

ONE

Today I started working for Julian again after a break of some years. It's part-time work, weather-dependent and badly paid, but it allows me time for my other preoccupations. I meet him in the farmyard where he is moving about with his usual grace, sorting out the few tools we will need during the day. He is still a handsome man, tall and rangy but now a little slimmer and with flecks of grey in the hair above his ears. We smile at each other and say good morning but he's taciturn and business-like at this time of day. We will talk later. Together we attach a harrow to the back of his tractor. While he's adjusting the three-point linkage I look around the farmyard. There are no livestock now as he's gone over entirely to growing organic vegetables. It's tidier and less smelly here than it was before. Opposite the farmhouse is a large barn and sticking out of the open doors is the bow of his boat, the half-restored yacht that he has been working on for so long. It doesn't look any closer to being in the water than when I last saw it.

Julian takes me down to the bottom field and sets me off on the tractor. The land has been ploughed and rotovated and now I must drive back and forth with the harrow to get the soil into perfect condition for planting. Most of Julian's land is open and exposed, with views across the rolling hills, but this field is sheltered, surrounded by overgrown hedges and strips of woodland. I'm hidden away from the rest of the world, absorbed in the pleasant monotony of driving slowly up and down. The countryside has changed in the last few weeks – there's abundance where before there was absence. There's more light and more colour, the greys of winter replaced by vibrant greens and the yellows and reds of flowers along the bottom of the hedge. When I get off the tractor to stretch my legs I'm aware of a great deal of birdsong. And the warmth of the sun is drawing up new smells from the ground.

There are a few hours of tractor-driving. I must be fairly well lost in day dreams because at one point in the morning I look behind me to see Julian perched on the harrow, crouching down and looking at the effect my work has on the soil. I didn't even see him come into the field. Now and again he snatches a handful of soil off the surface of the field and rubs it between his fingers. This is the Julian I remember, a great deal of knowledge, some sort of qualification in soil science I think, and beyond this a visceral passion for the land. And, incongruously, a pipe-dream sailing boat in his barn. I look behind a couple of times and he's still there contemplating the soil. Then he's mysteriously gone and I'm alone again.

At lunch-time I leave the tractor and walk up to the farmyard. The farm is quite a way up the hill but the buildings sit in a slight undulation of the land and are somewhat hidden by trees that are now coming into leaf. When I arrive Julian stops what he is doing and makes tea for the two of us. We sit outside in the sunshine, looking across at the barn and the boat, eating our lunch. It's warm enough, for the first time this year, to take off our shirts and bask in the sun. Perhaps I'm wrong in thinking Julian is slimmer than he was when I last saw him. I think it's my perception and what has happened is that I've put on weight again. I feel pale and flabby sitting next to him. Never mind, sunshine and manual labour will transform me back to the man I once was.

"I'd forgotten how nice it is too work outside," I say. "Thank-you for taking me on again."

Julian finishes his mouthful of sandwich. "It's okay. I'm glad you're enjoying it. I think it's good to have someone around who likes the work." He smiles. "It means I don't have to feel so guilty about not paying very much."

"I didn't see you come into the field and get on the harrow when I was driving along."

"I know, you were concentrating so hard on the tractor driving," he says, with no irony in his voice, just a hint of a smile.

"You haven't changed much you know."

"Neither have you," I say, an image in my mind of him crouched on the harrow, crumbling the soil between his fingers.

"Strange that your hobby is working on the boat. There's a sort of poetic incongruity to it, the boat sat there in the farmyard, so far from the sea."

"You really, really haven't changed. I see a boat, you see a poem," he shakes his head. "But the truth is I don't get much time to work on it. And I'll have to change the keel if I want to get in and out of the shallow harbours near here."

I've finished eating now and lean back against the wall with my eyes closed.

"One day I'll take you out in her," he says.

"You know your boat appeared in one of my attempts at writing," I say.

"I hope it was in the water and not in the barn."

"Oh yes. Sailed by a man who loved the land but escaped to the sea for a few days, travelling along a stretch of coastline in the west of Britain."

"I don't like you writing about me. You never said anything about this before."

"Don't worry, it's not you. It's someone maybe a little like me. I've just borrowed the boat."

"So this chap sails along the coast. What's the story?"

"He remembers a past love affair that took place along that coastline. He views it differently from the boat."

"Who's the woman?" Julian looks uncomfortable.

"She's tall and has black hair. She's no one you or I have ever known."

We don't speak again for a little while. There's a bird singing nearby in the hedge but it's hidden among the leaves and I can't see it no matter how hard I try. The sound is very beautiful but it also sounds teasing, ironic.

"What's that?" I ask Julian.

"A willow-warbler," he says. "It's very common around here.

It's a fine sound though, isn't it?"

Then I tell Julian about my first swim of the year. The sea was so full of brown and green seaweed churning in the waves that it was like bathing in cold soup.

"I don't know what makes the sea behave differently from one day to the next," I say.

"Changes in the waves," says Julian. I know he is about to give me a scientific explanation.

"Different waves scour different things up from the sea bed and sometimes they leave them on the beach and sometimes they take them away."

"So what makes the waves different?"

"Speed, fetch, and constancy."

"I'm sorry?" I smile.

"The factors determining the size of waves. The speed of the wind, of course. Fetch – how far the wind blows over the water. And constancy – how long it blows for."

"And leaving things on the beach?"

"Constructive waves and destructive waves – according to how often and how big. Wash and backswash."

"Wash and backswash," I say, "Speed, fetch and constancy. I think it's you who's the poet around here."

When we have finished eating and are about to go back to work I tell Julian that I might start working on the story again.

"The story about no one you or I have ever known," he smiles. "What's it to be called?"

"*The Land as Viewed from the Sea.*"

He's the first person I've told about it.

After lunch we go back down to the bottom field. I take a break from tractor driving and we work together, marking out the beds that we will fill with small cabbage plants. This involves firming the ground either side of each bed by simply treading the soil down as we walk up and down the field. To walk parallel to each other at the appropriate distance we must each hold onto the end of a short piece of wood that Julian has brought down to the field for this purpose. Surely there must be a more efficient way of doing this. I feel daft. I imagine the scene as viewed from afar – a landscape of fields and scattered woodlands, only an occasional sign of human activity: a tractor moving across the scene here and there maybe, and in one field two men walking up and down the cultivated land holding onto each end of a piece of wood, the connection between them a carefully measured distance.

Then we are planting out the seedlings. Bent over in the sunshine we make holes in the soft soil with our fingers, drop the plants in, firm them and move on. We talk a little about old times and our plans for the future. Julian is as enthusiastic about his few acres as he has ever been. It's good working together again. There's a long pause while he thinks hard about something. Then he has a question to ask me.

"If you do carry on with the story," he says, "will you let me read some of it?"

A man is at the helm of a boat far out in the bay. The boat is keeling over in a strong side-wind so that he stands as on a hillside. The salt spray wets his bare legs. He must work to keep the vessel on course despite its pitch and roll in the swell. He's aiming at a distant hill on the coast in the north of the bay but leeway (the sideways drift of the boat with the wind) will take him to a different point along the coast. Below the hill is a small seaside town that he can't yet see over the horizon. There's dark water all around, a sense of speed and a need to concentrate but still the motion and noise are conducive to reverie and something like hallucination. He smells vivid smells that cannot be there. Yesterday it was the scent of her, suddenly, as if she were standing by his side. Not even consciously thinking of her at all and then a smell as concrete, vivid and tangible as any sensation of his actual surroundings. Today, with a particular seaside town just over the horizon, he can smell the house in which she lived. Cold, odourless waves surround him, slapping against the side of the boat and stretching for miles in every direction. And he smells the inside of a house.

What did they do there? Only talk and make love. Both activities with a child-like excitement and abandon. So much to say; and the sense of being with someone who genuinely wants to hear and understand. But sometimes she's talking and he can't hear a word. Just watching her takes up all his mental faculties. Like in a silent film he sees her mouth moving and her smile between sentences. She can smile at will he's noticed. Under any circumstances she can achieve a perfectly plausible and, of course, beautiful smile. But now this is the real smile, quite different, with a deep curve to her bottom lip. She's stopped speaking and he's looking at the way her hair lies across her forehead.

"You're not listening again," she says.

"No, I'm sorry. Thinking how beautiful you are uses up all my energy."

She hits him with a cushion and smiles at his nonsense. He kisses her just below her earlobe. And on the delicate bones of her shoulder. Now they are not talking. They undress each other silently and begin to make love. Unintentionally she lets out a particularly passionate sigh and simultaneously they realise how absurd and crazy they sound, like some bad romantic movie. They explode into laughter.

He's on a boat, a ketch with full sail up and a tendency to turn into the wind. Somehow he can control this thing despite the vivid memories. He can feel the muscles of his face softened into a smile and he has the beginnings of an erection, surely at the most useless and inappropriate time of his life. This is not what he came here to do. He's pointing the boat at a place he can't see, isn't really travelling towards and doesn't want to visit. He's smiling happily at the thought of someone he's learnt to hate.

He puts on the self-steering gear and goes below to the charts. Perhaps he can sail close past the town and along the coast to the marina before nightfall. It was a special place to him once, that town. He has never viewed it from the sea.

On the deck again he sets a new course by the compass. The town is still over the horizon but he can see it anyway. He can see a curving promenade by a castle and two people sitting on a bench looking out to sea. They are very still, reflective, immersed in the presence of each other, the space between them a tangible connection. Small, glassy waves are breaking on the sand, their crests blowing back neatly in the off-shore wind. The couple are discussing waves.

"Speed, fetch, and constancy – the three things that make the waves," he says.

"Like three dogs." She smiles a dreamy smile.

"Sea-dogs," he says and gives them commands, "Lie still Constancy, Run Speed, and... "

"And what?"

"Fetch, Fetch." They laugh.

"I love your words," she says.

She's looking at him with an intense serious expression. She kisses him.

"I like this bit here," she says and runs her finger along his upper lip then leans forward, gently taking this momentarily favourite part of him between her tongue and her own upper lip. For a while they are oblivious to their surroundings. If the sea quietly drained away they wouldn't miss it.

Now they move away from each other and are lost in their own thoughts. After a while he turns and looks at her. The breeze is blowing her long hair forward across her face and she reaches up with both hands, twists the dark strands into a tangle, and tucks it to one side. Her movements are both graceful and awkward, feminine and practical. He can see that she is smiling to herself.

"What are you thinking of now?" he asks.

"You really want to know?"

He nods his head.

"I'm thinking about when you couldn't stay the night last

time. As you drove away I sat on the toilet listening to your car going down the lane."

"Yes?"

"And I watched your come dripping into the water and making pretty patterns. Do you see? Everything about you is beautiful."

They move close together and he sees her eyes moving from side to side, scanning his face with concentration. He realises that he must be doing the same. They kiss. Then they turn towards the sea.

"You know the way the bay curves round here?" she says. "It's like a big amphitheatre. All the way around there are people looking in from beaches and cliff-tops."

"But there's an empty stage," he says, "there's nothing out there."

"Is that why we like it?" she says. "We can people it with our own imaginings. I don't know. I do know you bring out such daft thoughts in me. And you with your Speed, Fetch and Constancy."

He thinks for a moment. "You know I'm more creative when I'm with you. I wouldn't talk about these things with anyone else. And this is what I like best. When it's just you and me."

"Which means you're glad my brother's gone."

There is a very quick change in her mood. A move towards anger that he recognises from experience.

"I didn't say that," he says.

"It's the truth though, isn't it?"

"I like it when it's just the two of us."

Their conversation comes to an awkward close. She gets up and walks off across the road. He waits. The light fades and the sound of waves breaking on the beach seems louder. When she returns it is with two cans of beer one of which she has already opened. She sits and lights a cigarette.

"You're such a filthy hedonist," he says, but in a tone of admiration.

She is smiling a cool straight-lipped smile. He can't be sure that she is happy.

It's another hot day and Julian and I are planting again. The warmth brings out odours from the vegetation and soil. We are working very fast along the beds, the sun hot on our bare shoulders and backs. There are long silences. Even the birdsong is subdued as the day heightens.

Before lunch we shower. The outside shower is rigged up from a tap at the back of the barn, the one in which Julian keeps the boat. We are out of sight of the farmyard and the land drops away gently below us to fields, hedgerows, woods. Between the trees you can see the lane to the farm. It's very hot here. We take turns to strip off and stand under the shower in the bright sunshine.

"You've put some of my words into your lovers' mouths," Julian says, concerned.

"I did it on purpose. To show how it's only a story."

Julian is standing naked with the spray of water hitting his shoulders and running down his back. He is tanned and muscular from working outdoors. Particles of soil are being washed down to his feet and onto the concrete path. I look away across the fields. After a while he turns off the shower.

"You make it seem true – that only she brings out those words in him." He seems petulant, jealous.

"It's only a story, okay? *The Land as Viewed from the Sea* is only a story. None of this is real."

TWO

Julian's neighbours are connected to the main road by a different lane so we take a short cut across the fields. We're walking alongside a tangled hedgerow and looking out across a small valley to the fields on the opposite side. All the land here is under grass but it's not uniform. Most of the fields on the slope in front of us have been grazed short by sheep or cattle, but one has been left to grow for hay. This field right ahead is moving in the wind while all the rest are still. The wind blows up the slope and moves the long grass in wave-like patterns, each new breeze bending the green blades to show their silvery undersides for a moment. The effect is strange and mesmeric. Like a picture the landscape is still, except for one square field in the centre of the scene which is filled with a continuous flowing movement of silver and green. This holds our attention. We are looking at a window through which we can see a more fluid and dreamlike version of the world. We stand still and don't speak for a while. We are both smiling.

Julian's lent me his shirt and trousers for the day as the work is going to be dirtier than I imagined. I'm a little shorter and broader than he is but the clothes fit well. So I'm a different man for the day, incognito, like a disguised lover in a play. Now we turn along the valley, look at a different view, and are able to talk. There's a sound like an overgrown grasshopper coming from a large thorn-tree standing alone in the field. Julian tells me that it's a yellowhammer and its call apparently sounds like the words 'a little bit of bread and no cheese'.

"But country hospitality demands something more sumptuous on a day like this. You'll see. I think you will like the Cranbournes. Olivia is a solicitor but today she'll play the part of farmer's wife to perfection. Gareth, the husband, is a very good man. Only he can be taciturn like you'd expect a farmer to be."

On the way up to their farm I notice the countryside is changing. The vibrant greens of spring are darkening and the early spring flowers are disappearing under the coarser, more vigorous vegetation of nettles and hogweed. Swifts are screaming overhead as we approach the farm.

By the time we arrive things are almost set up for the day's shearing. Maybe two hundred ewes are penned in the big shed and the smell of fresh urine and dung has begun to accumulate. Just inside the wide doors the contractors have unfolded their special trailer into a temporary platform and the three of them are carefully going over their equipment. They are from New Zealand. Strong, perfectly made young men, they stretch and limber-up on their stage, like three athletes preparing for competition. They wear soft shoes with no soles or edges, special shearers' trousers, and singlets bearing the names of outfits or places they've worked in their home country. I guess that is Olivia who's offering them coffee that she's brought down from the house. She's older than the shearers of course but an attractive woman with bobbed blond hair and a mildly flirtatious manner. The young men take their coffee, their eyes betraying no interest in her. Gareth, her burly husband, welcomes us and shows us to our station – a table a little away from the shearing platform where we are to roll the fleeces into tight bundles.

It turns out to be a foul job but an interesting spectacle. The shearers are indeed athletes, working very fast and skillfully. Everything revolves around the need to keep them supplied with sheep and get the fleeces away and packed. As each shorn ewe tumbles off the platform and runs out of the door into sunlight another is pushed out of a small holding-pen into its place. Other ewes are pushed up through the pens to keep the supply going. The stench increases. My hands and the front of all my clothes are coated in sheep grease. It is hard to keep up with the flow and all sense of the world outside is lost.

The centre of our actions is the shearing platform and the three men working on it. The rest of us are audience and stage hands. Olivia comes in occasionally to watch, drawn despite the noise, the smell, and the seemingly casual ill-treatment of the ewes. From time to time Julian and I have to move a huge sack full of rolled fleeces and replace it with an empty one. The full sack is always heavy and awkward. There's a connectedness when the two of us have to lift a weight together. Sometimes it is eye-contact, sometimes body language, that says a wordless 'okay, lift now', and is followed by our co-ordinated movement.

It turns into a very long morning of tedious work. I'm willing to day-dream but Julian has less ability than me in that department – he wants to talk to me about geology, of all things. I'm only half-listening to him talk of continents moving about, new oceans appearing, rocks being formed. It's too factual and scientific for me but some of it goes in.

At lunchtime we wash in a large tub of hot water by the back door of the farmhouse and go in to eat. There is a crowd of us around the long table, with Gareth at one end and Olivia, when she's not bringing in the food, at the other. There's a sense of tradition, of some baronial banquet – maybe that's Arthur and Guinivere presiding over the feast. Certainly Olivia has a strength of personality and holds court, leading the conversation. Stories of farm life and of different animals they have owned lead us gently towards talking of the world of human affairs.

Olivia tells the story from their early years when all their milking cows had names. One cow, Maisy, was way down the cows' butting-order (their hierarchy) but when she had a calf and was allowed to see it every day after milking, it gave her an incentive to be brave. She would push her way through the others, fearless of cows who had once intimidated her. And this newfound bravery gave her status for the rest of her life.

"So an event in her life changed her forever. It's the same for all of us I think. Does anyone have any life-changing stories they would like to share? Something from the past that's left a mark?"

She is centre-stage now. She looks around the room for an answer. The shearers are drawn in by her animation but seem to sense that they are out of their depth with her. She smiles at Julian but he says nothing. I am interested in the past but it doesn't seem as simple for me as it was for Maisy the cow. I look across at Olivia.

"We change our perceptions of the past. It's not solid. I think the past is a dream and you can undream or re-dream or change it. And change the present at the same time."

She looks at me carefully, "Is this some sort of personal preoccupation for you?" she asks.

"Maybe." I feel conspicuous and suddenly shy. Julian helps me out.

"I think I know what you mean," he says. "It's like archaeology, my brother is an archaeologist and I know that they are very careful where they dig. As soon as you unearth the past you destroy it. Or change it to something it never was."

At the end of the table Gareth looks like he wants to keep silent but can't help but speak, "I can't change my past. Nothing can change it. Some of it was a nightmare for me and for those unlucky enough to be around me. Until I gave up drinking that is. But I'm pleased with my present."

Olivia is smiling at the other end of the table. Happy to have drawn us out a little. Maybe proud of her husband. But we are all uncomfortable with getting deep and personal. There is a feeling of relief as we get back to talk of the land and of Julian, his organic methods of growing, and his passion for wildlife.

"Did you notice when the council mowed all the bluebells up the lane a couple of weeks ago?" Olivia asks.

"Yes I noticed alright," Julian says.

"You never said anything at the time."

Julian shrugs his shoulders, "I was too angry to even speak about it."

Olivia gives him a curious sympathetic look.

When Julian and I are walking back across the fields in the evening I ask him about Olivia and Gareth.

"They seem a good couple, happy together."

"All couples seem like that from the outside," he says.

"Meaning?"

"Only that Gareth is addicted to work. He has no time for anything else. Did you see the bird-scarer in his garden? A little wooden figure that turns a windmill. Well Gareth is like that. He turns the handle all the time and keeps the thing moving. Then you look again and you realise that actually it's moving him."

"That's a nice little metaphor. Can I use that in my writing?"

"You can if you want. It's funny working with you now you're a writer. Anything I say might get put into a story."

"I'm not really a writer. And I shouldn't be doing it – it's taking me away from my art work. There's a couple of exhibitions I'm meant to be preparing for."

"Well, it's interesting for me, the way you mess with reality."

"I'm afraid I don't have a strong interest in the concept of reality."

"So you say John, so you always say. If I told you all I know about poor old Gareth you might think again – about his drinking days, I mean. If you'd been where he'd been you'd have a healthy interest in reality alright."

I think I sometimes feel a little superior to Julian. His explanations seem too rational, too simple. He's trained in the sciences. It makes me feel that I'm looking for deeper meanings that can't be easily put into words. Then at times his voice takes on a certain tone, a quiet understanding manner. And I feel he knows some things that I have yet to learn.

Today it's not smells but music. Another direct route to the unconscious. He has been cruising along the coast using the inboard diesel engine to power the boat. No sail up today because there's very little wind, just flukey breezes. The boat behaves badly without sail, rolling in the swell. The sun comes out from time to time, casting patches of shimmering light on the dark water or highlighting a stretch of hills along the coast. Again his thoughts are going to unanticipated places and scenes. Memories that should hold no power over his emotions anymore take over his thoughts, fill his understimulated landless day. He can love sailing but sometimes he misses the intricate detail of the land. Instead of the calm, meditative state that the sea sometimes brings out in him, today he has a feeling of sensory deprivation. So imagination fills the spaces.

He turns on the radio; it's not tuned into a station, no sound comes out. But that's not what he hears. Following straight on from the click of the switch he hears music, a track from an album he heard often enough with her, a loud voice over electric guitar chords: '*If it makes you happy, it can't be that bad, if it makes you happy then why the hell are you so sad?*' Not great words, but it was their song at the end – always one of them asking the other, "Why the hell are you so sad?" The music sounds loud in his head, more real than the silence. Is it the rolling of the boat that knots his stomach? No, there are other symptoms too, and after all this time, not sea-sick but love-sick. Unbelievable.

He doesn't recognise the coast here. It looks bleaker and emptier than it should. But as he approaches a small town he can see a valley. Just a fold in the hill, a little line running down to the stony beach.

The lovers are on the beach by the entrance of a steep sided gully that carries a stream down from the hills. They are collecting pieces of driftwood and shells left behind by last night's big tide. A little way into the gully a long driftwood branch has become jammed. It looks like some sinuous beached sea-monster. They walk up to it and she moves around it taking photographs. Then she scrapes some coloured mud from the stream side and smears war-paint lines on her cheeks. She turns and faces him, grinning. He has to push her camera to one side a little to kiss her. They are interrupted by a wolf-whistle from above.

Stretched across the gully a little way up-stream are two steel girders. A new footbridge is being built for the coast path. There are three men up there working on it and now looking down on the two below them. The men walk across the girders from time to time carrying pieces of equipment or timbers on their shoulders. It's a forty foot drop to the stream bed below but the men seem unconcerned. She walks up the gully balancing on the wet rocks and is now photographing them as they cross. Crouching into the bank she experiments with different angles. Sometimes she is directly below the girders, photographing the shapes the men and their loads make against the sky. The men are flattered by her attention and are joking loudly, self-conscious. Now they have to carry something like a heavy railway sleeper. Two men are going to cross together, one on each girder, the timber held between them. They seem nervous but it's clear they have done it before. They get the load comfortable and begin counting, "one two, one two", setting a rhythm. They make eye contact at the right moment and set off together, walking in step and still counting out loud. They are aware of being watched and of the slight ludicrousness of what they are doing. So it is that one man changes to "two one, two one" half-way across, on impulse, as a joke. His colleague pauses in his step and immediately the timber is at an angle and difficult to hold onto. They are at the point where the drop below them is at its greatest. They manage to stop simultaneously. They are unsteady for a moment. Then one man takes command of the situation, gives clear instructions, and they level out, start the count again, and pace together the rest of the way across.

The couple below walk out towards the sea, a little tense. He is angry with her.

"You'd make a good photojournalist. Forget this arty stuff, you seem to always be about where accidents happen." He had intended to be humorous but there was a bitter edge to his voice.

"So I'm always where accidents happen am I? And you're always the first to criticise."

"I'm sorry. It was a scary moment. I was really frightened just then and it made me angry. They were stupid to mess about like that."

They walk along the shore to where large slabs of grey mudstone have fallen from the cliffs onto the rocky wave-cut platform below. Where one of the slabs has split open a perfect fossilised ripple pattern is revealed.

"I wanted to show you this," he says, "these are the ripple marks left by a retreating tide of a different sea millions of years ago. And instead of getting washed out by the next tide they got preserved for all this time. Strange isn't it? It was so long ago – all the things alive then have since become extinct and all the things alive now didn't yet exist. And the continents were different. The atmosphere was different. And something as ephemeral as wave marks on the sand got preserved. Weird."

"I still like to hear you talk about things," she says, "you can make something that might be boring come really alive." She looks at him admiringly.

He accepts her compliment. It is a happy normality for them to put each other on pedestals, to be excited about each other's ideas, to be continually giving and learning. Until a huge part of each person is their experience of the other. They stand together in that strange world of lovers, exaggeratedly focussed on each other, oblivious of the world around them.

"Half of me is you," he says very seriously.

"Whatever," she says, smiling at his earnestness. Perhaps she understands. She lets go of his hand and sits down on one of the slabs.

"What makes things last?" she says. "I'm always asking myself that."

She has loaded another film into her camera and photographs the slabs and the ripple marks. She is absorbed again in what she is doing and has to ask him to move out of the way for a certain shot. He sits on the stones and waits for her.

"I don't understand," she says, "about the mud at the edge of the sea being fossilised but still being by the sea."

"But it hasn't been by the sea all this time. The continents have moved and the ocean where this mud was deposited got squeezed into oblivion by two land masses colliding. Then the continents spread apart again and a new sea arrived."

She's looking at the world through the camera lens again. He doesn't know if she's listening to him but he goes on anyway.

"Geologists call the old ocean the Iapetus Sea. Iapetus was one of the titans from Greek myth. They were big guys, the titans, and when they came out of the pub after a skin-full they would move a few continents about. Make some new mountains."

"I never thought I would go out with a man who spouted geology at me. But it's okay, you make it lively, poetic even."

"Only okay?" he asks.

"Very, very okay, if you need to know. In fact I think we should do a book together, *Geology for Poets*. You write and I'll do the photographs."

She sounds excited. He wishes she would put the camera away and look towards him.

Back on the promenade they find out the time.

"Do you realise that it took two hours to walk that tiny way?" He points back to the bridge over the gully.

"That's really strange," she says. "You know we don't have the same relationship with time that everyone else has."

"Poor them," he says. " The unlovers. I can't imagine being on Planet Unlover now. Or being here without you."

"Me too," she says, looking around at the other people.

They sit down on a bench and look out at the sea. It is now

getting towards evening, the air still and the sun half-obscured by thin cloud. The sea appears to have its own light coming from below or within and glows with a metallic sheen.

"It looks otherworldly to me," he says. " I don't think you can take a picture of that, can you?"

There's a long pause during which her face clouds over with a frown.

"I hate it when you don't understand my art," she says. "It's the most important thing to me."

"Perhaps I do understand a little. But because you take such care to get certain images I think you're trying to capture the real scene. And then you take the photographs and work on them and distort them with a computer or wrap them up in a painting until there's nothing much left of the original. So I wonder why you took such care in the first place. Or you produce a series that tell a story that never happened. Or paint something that seems unrelated to what you started out with."

She watches him very carefully as he speaks.

"Then I realise what you're doing. That you capture a feeling, a sense of what was there for you. And I understand that that is more realistic in a way than any apparently accurate picture. I mean, that's all we have really. Our perceptions. Feelings."

She is radiant, smiling as if he's making love to her.

"I think you really do understand a little. You wonderful man."

Her eyes light up and she looks childishly happy. There is a strange deep curve to her lower lip as she smiles.

"Let's have some food and then a serious drink," she says.

In the evening after the pub shuts they walk out to the bridge along the new path. She brings her camera and a tripod. Perhaps the moon has come round enough to shine on the girders or on the waterfall behind. The three men have camped on the other side and are drinking and singing around a fire. He watches while she scrambles around the slippery edges trying to take photographs. She is quite drunk. She looks across at the men illuminated by the flames.

"I'm going across to see them," she says cheerfully. Of course he argues. The girders are high and a wind is blowing in gusts off the sea. He has plenty of reasons for not wanting her to go across.

"You're so, so mad," he says very seriously.

"I need to take some more pictures," she says, "this is what I do."

He has to watch her slender figure swaying a little, the camera and tripod over her shoulder, as she starts out onto the bridge. Perhaps the girders are as much as a foot wide, it is really very easy. But he's feeling sick with fear as she moves out to where the drop is greatest. The wind gusts and blows her hair across her face for a while. She stops until it subsides. He is aware of the sound of waves now breaking against the rocks at the bottom of the gully where they had been earlier in the day. He doesn't look down. Half way across she is visible in the moonlight and the singing from the fireside has stopped. The three men make their way down to their end of the bridge and one reaches out and takes her hand as she arrives.

He waits for her to look back and wave but she goes with the men up to the fire. He watches for a while expecting her to take photographs. He can see figures around a fire, the glow of cigarettes, and two tents. And perhaps her profile, head tilted back, drinking from a wine bottle.

She doesn't come back to the flat until the early hours of the morning and sets the dogs barking. He hasn't slept. He wants to hear words some words of apology, something like, "I'm sorry if I worried you. Thank you for letting me be me."

But she collapses onto the other bed in silence. She smells

strongly of drink. Later he awakes to the sound of her throwing up in the wash-basin.

Julian and I are hoeing weeds out of a crop of leeks on a long slope up the curve of the hill. The rows stretch up the slope and disappear over the near horizon. He works faster than I do and we only speak momentarily when he comes down the hill to start on a new row. He is preoccupied with something, his anger translates into furious action and I feel guilty that I can't keep up with his pace. Only at lunchtime can we talk, sitting on the top of the hill looking out over the landscape. There's a skylark singing overhead. A tiny triangle of sea is visible through a gap in the hills.

"I read the passage you gave me last night before I went to sleep. There's not much of it. But it must have touched a nerve with me. When I began working with you this morning I started getting angry with your photographer woman for her behaviour. It's silly isn't it?"

There's more to this. A few words on a piece of paper shouldn't rile him. It's strange that my story affects his mood so much. He doesn't want to talk and I take a notebook out of my bag.

"Oh no, not more words."

There seems nothing I can say to ease his irritation with the world today. I think for a while. Then I write a little, tear the page from the book and pass it over for him to read. After lunch he works at a more relaxed pace. Then he stops and leans on his hoe smiling at something.

He shouts across the slope to me, "Am I going mad or is it you?"

She arrives back at the flat shortly after him, she hadn't stayed long at the campfire. She slips out of her clothes and gets into the bed beside him.

"I'm really sorry if I worried you going over there like that. Thank you for letting me be me."

THREE

The sea is a desert today, a uniformly barren expanse stretching away from him on all sides. No sign of life. The sun is reflected off the water and his eyes narrow against the glare. He is alone, far out in the bay, the shore barely visible through the summer haze. He misses trees. He finds that he wants leaves, many leaves to filter the sunlight and dapple him with their shade. The colour green, the presence of earth. He imagines lying on the grass between the trees with another person's warm skin against his own. He wants to lie naked and be kissed all over his body. Kisses on his mouth, shoulders, chest and stomach. And to lie on his front and have wet kisses down his back. The warm wet of lips and tongue against his muscles. The sea is dry.

The tuning peg won't stay and the top string of the cello goes repeatedly out of pitch. She pushes her long hair back away from her face and tries again. Someone in the room says that it's a presentiment of discord, a premonition. The instrument is sensitive to the human condition. They are all seated together in a circle with their music stands, flute, oboe, classical guitar, violin and cello. The hopelessly amateur mediaeval music group. He can't get a strong enough tone out of the wooden flute and changes it for his modern, metal one. He plays a few phrases while, opposite him, she tries to adjust her instrument. Then her eyes light up with mischief.

"I'm going to scandalise you all. Please give it a go – just once as we're at my place tonight."

She puts the cello in the corner and has picked up an electric bass guitar and now half-sits on, half-leans against the amplifier in the corner of the room. She switches it on, plays a few notes and adjusts tone and volume. People are smiling, apart from the oboe player who is shaking his head. They play sedate dance tunes with strange harmonies. There's a stronger flute and a punchier bass-line now. He is playing the flute and trying not to smile – it will spoil his embouchure and he'll fluff the note. But she looks so different playing bass. She's lost the solemn look and is now laid back, smiling. He searches for the word in his head as they play the repeat. Is she funky or spunky or raunchy? It's too late, he's smiling and his lips have gone and the notes won't come out. They finish the piece without him while he just sits, smiles and watches her.

It is later, between pieces, that she starts to play a jazz riff as the others arrange their music. He puts his flute to his lips and improvises over it. Just gently flowing runs of notes. Then he's moving up the register and playing with more rhythm. Improvisation is magic when it works and it begins to work now. He plays a slow accompaniment for her to have a chance to elaborate. Then she's back to the riff, punching out the notes. There are only two people in the room. She looks him in the eye, daring him. And he hits the upper register, fast phrases and long inspired downward speeding runs. They are lovers already.

But it is a long time before they know it. People around are surprised at how long it takes to happen. There are many times when they are in company that other people seem to disappear from the scene. They are in the pub with the music group and there are two people suddenly in intense dialogue across the table. Perhaps they are talking about a film they have both seen or a book they have read. The people around them have dropped out of the conversation and look at each other with knowing smiles. Sometimes they are arguing, a sort of intellectual sparring that seems to be about disagreement but is a testing of each other. Eventually, by chance, they are alone together. They are in her house waiting for a lift that never materialises. When he first comes in she avoids eye contact. They spend a great deal of energy talking of nothing and avoiding silences. The very first expression of anything between them comes after a long pause in a forced conversation. They have not touched. They have admitted nothing. She has moved onto the sofa where he is sitting so they can both see an illustration in a book that they are not interested in. He says one small sentence:

"We're much more than friends, aren't we?"

She will not answer. She looks away.

"It's true isn't it? Say something. Tell me I'm crazy."

Eventually she looks at him. Resigned, smiling.

"I'm crazy too."

Now they are lovers. "I'm crazy too," she said and they kissed. And now he's walking along the promenade to her flat to see if it's true and not a dream. Last night was a transformation. They were lovers in the way they spoke to each other, not just in the words but in their tone of voice. People who are not lovers don't speak like that. They were lovers in their body language even when not touching. They were lovers with their eyes. Their hands, when they did touch, expressed their feelings for one another. For part of the evening they lay side by side together on the rug in front of the fire, both of them fully clothed, and they had talked excitedly and looked into each other's eyes. He now has the banal realisation that he's long-sighted, when her face was close to his she was out of focus, indistinct, too close to see properly. Mostly today he has had a physical memory, non-visual like a scent, of the warmth of their clothed and half-clothed bodies against each other. They didn't actually make love. That's strange because he knows that they are lovers if ever any two people were.

He stops and sits on a bench looking towards the sea. He will wait and be exactly on time, she said five o'clock. The wide promenade is popular at this time of day and busy even though it is not the holiday season. Behind him he can hear the carefree voices of people walking past, enjoying the sunshine after a spell of cool wet weather. He can hear the traffic on the road and is aware of the buildings on the other side, a row of big Victorian houses with bay windows. One of these houses has a newly painted red door. It is a profoundly significant place in the small town, her flat is upstairs, perhaps she is looking out from the window now and hoping to see him. He looks at the beach and the waves breaking. Small shadows of clouds pass across the green and grey and blue surface of the water. The sea, as it sometimes does, has redecorated the beach overnight. The tide has taken away the rubbish and driftwood and left the grey stones clean, just touched here and their by a little pink seaweed on the strand-line. He's not at all surprised to see that the material world has been affected by their change. Five o'clock. It feels like no other moment in time has had such profound significance. Five o'clock is crucial, momentous. He feels like an excited schoolboy and when he rings her door-bell he is nervous. Their second time together as transformed people.

She opens the door and turns away without looking at him. But when she is in her room with the door shut she starts to talk excitedly about times in their recent past that now stand out with vivid importance. The time he took her side in an argument, said a kind thank you, touched her on the arm to point out something. When she leaves him for a moment to go to the bathroom he looks around the room. She has left out a book that he once lent her. Her bass guitar and cello lean in the corner. A half-finished painting and some photographs are taped to a board against the wall. In the wash basin are her paintbrushes and reflected in the mirror above is his face looking ten years younger. He smiles at himself, a smile that he doesn't remember seeing before. She comes back into the room and stands beside him so that they can see the reflection of the two of them side by side.

"Your face is back to front but mine is the right way round – why is that?" he says, teasing.

"My face is the way it's always been thank you. It's yours that's all wrong." She turns him towards her, "What kind of a man am I falling in love with? When I leave the room he stands and looks at himself in the mirror."

"Are we lovers?" he asks.

"I told a few people today that we are," she says. "It'll be all round town by now. It had better be true."

When they are both naked she walks across the room and puts a record on loud, a jazz album that he would normally dislike.

"I'm a noisy lover," she says. "I don't want everyone to hear us," and she pulls him towards her.

In those early days they would be crazy with excitement together. Perhaps he would come into her room while she was painting and she would put her brush down quietly, kiss him and they would make love without speaking. Or they would be lost in a torrent of words and ideas, literature, music, their childhoods, old lovers. They would be astonished at the closeness of their visions of the world and how it worked. They would be delighted by the differences, the things they had to give to each other. And things that would be unacceptable in someone else would be wonderful in a lover. They would lose track of time, making love at any hour of the day or night. Forgetting to eat and then feasting at some strange time. Their love itself was a potent aphrodisiac, giving them energy that they had never known with anyone else. They were young in love. The little thinning of his hair, the first grey strands in hers, these things didn't carry the meaning that they would have for others.

"The more I give, the more I have," she says. "It's from Romeo and Juliet. It's true isn't it? Why are you smiling?"

"I know it's ridiculous but sometimes when we're making love I feel like we're two young lovers. I actually feel very young. As if with my first love. Stupid isn't it?"

"Sometimes I feel that too," she says.

"And you look at me and tell me that I'm beautiful; no woman has said that to me before. And I look in the mirror and see the lines on my face and I think – what's this all about? It makes me laugh. I can see the truth but I'm happy anyway. I can't believe you said I looked like a film star." He shakes his head, smiling, bemused.

She is nodding seriously. Then she smiles and looks mischievous.

"But I didn't tell you which film star. Maybe it was Jimmy Cagney – no, no I'm teasing. You are beautiful. You are young. Today."

On the boat his stomach aches as if starved. Right now he cannot eat. He hadn't planned this but he has a startlingly clear vision of her face in front of him. He doesn't need this. All around him the water is dark and inhospitable. There is a strong wind on the starboard beam that keels the boat over and pushes it fast through the waves. He concentrates at the wheel, correcting the boat's course as it plunges forwards. He looks towards the land, green fields sloping down to grey cliffs at the sea's edge.

They are on the narrowest part of a remote stony beach at high tide. The cliffs here have been worn into smooth hollows by the action of stormy seas. She is half-leaning, half-sitting against the protruding base of the cliff, smiling at him, letting the wind blow her hair back away from her face.

"You're in the same position as when you're leaning back on your amp playing bass," he says. And after watching her some more. "Something I haven't told you before. When you play the bass your face takes on the same expressions as when you're making love. Well, some of the expressions."

The wind is pushing her clothes against her body. Her mouth is moving in speech but the waves are crashing on the stones behind and the sound is echoing off the cliff-face so that he can't hear. He must move his face close to hers. Too close to not kiss. His eyes are shut and the only sensations he has are of their mouths together and of the sound of the sea. As he moves his head from side to side the wave noise seems to roll around them. A cacophony of wet pebbles and foam with their bodies at the centre, spinning slowly. After a while she puts her mouth to his ear, "I want your sweet eloquent cock inside me."

It is one of those times when she doesn't put her hand to her mouth to stifle her cries. Deep radiant smiles and expressions of something like pain but not pain.

And then afterwards they gradually become aware of being watched. A seal is riding the waves quite close to the shore, his brown eyes fixed on them, curious. He pushes himself up on the swell to get a clearer view. She stands and calls to him, wordless sounds that she thinks will draw him closer. Only when she raises her arms does he drop below the surface, emerging a little further out, still watching them.

That night they are in her room, in bed together. He is naked but she wears a white cotton night-dress, old and softened by many washes. His hand is under the night-dress, against her side.

"Why eloquent?" he asks.

"Everything you do when we make love feels like you're telling me something very clearly."

Her eyes have softened.

"It's true," he says, "my hands have never been so alive, so expressive. And you're right it's not only my hands."

And then they are making love again, her night-dress is around her waist. He is pushing hard again and again as if to hurt her. It does not hurt.

"This is how much I love you" he says.

Julian and I run up from the field as the sky darkens. Before we reach the farmyard the first heavy drops of rain are falling and there is a flash of lightning over the hill. There's a rumble of thunder now and the rain is heavier. I'm very hot from running and the rain feels good on my bare shoulders and back. We are laughing like children when we run into the nearest building, Julian's barn. We sit on a plank of wood beside the boat, our backs against the wooden hull, the rainwater running from our bodies onto the dusty floor. I realise the incongruity of our position.

"Do you know we're sheltering from the rain under a boat?" I ask. "This is a new one for me."

When we have both got our breath back he wants to talk about my story.

"Has it ever been like that for you?" he asks.

The rain falls outside, dripping off the points of leaves, filling puddles in the farmyard. The air has the smell of summer rain after sunshine.

"I don't know. You dig up the past, idealise it, make it into fiction. Lose it in the process." I shrug my shoulders. I'm prevaricating. He asks again,

"Was it like that?"

"Yes... pretty much."

"I'm sorry."

We can hear the tree tops being pushed about by gusts of wind. Rain is being flung against the side of the barn. We won't be working outside again today. What does he mean – he's sorry?

"I'm beginning to wish that I wasn't reading your tale."

"Does that mean you're going to give me the sack?"

He laughs, "No don't worry about that. Only I don't know if I should stop reading it. Or perhaps it's too late. No, I don't think I can stop now if you're still willing. Anyway isn't it strange for you? You're telling me all this stuff."

"All this fiction," I remind him.

"But it isn't entirely fiction. We both know that. And you're destroying something as you unearth it. Do you remember I spoke about my brother who's an archaeologist? He says that when you dig up the past you destroy it. Doesn't that matter to you?"

I can hear a hard bitter tone in my voice as I answer him. I don't like it. I know it's masking sadness.

"No, I'm okay with that," I say, "It doesn't matter anymore."

FOUR

The sea is really not much fun. Also he has slept on the boat several nights in a row. Twice he stayed in the marina which is a large characterless carpark for boats, his anonymity there the only comfort. Once he tied up in a small harbour right next to the yacht club. He didn't want to speak to yachties so he cooked on board and sat on the harbour wall for a while. He slept in the forward cabin and awoke in the night. The tide had gone out leaving the harbour dry and the boat at a curious angle so that he was on a slope, at the bottom of which his head was pushed awkwardly against a bulkhead. So this evening he ties to a mooring buoy and goes ashore in the little inflatable to find a comfortable bed on dry land. It feels good rowing away from the boat. He's on a part of the coast that holds no memories, he's safe.

On the harbour-side he is questioned by Customs and Excise, two uniformed men and a woman who have just got out of a powerful launch. They have the right to search his vessel and look at his charts. But he's so obviously relaxed and innocent of wrong-doing that they quickly lose interest. He doesn't have to explain his erratic course along the coast. He walks into the town and finds a small bed-and-breakfast away from the sea.

In the pub that evening he discovers that his encounter with the authorities has given him a tiny amount of notoriety, just enough to get him bought a pint and be introduced to the strange mixture of locals and incomers that meet there. The people here are mildly eccentric and good to be with. As the evening progresses he becomes outgoing, ebullient, making people laugh, and pleased enough to be with others to be good listener too. It is very much what he needs. It puts the nonsense of the last few days into perspective. The memories, reopening of old wounds, the self-enforced loneliness, it's all unnecessary. Tonight he's back in the present; with real people in the real world.

Later, in the bed-and-breakfast, he falls asleep, pleasantly drunk and with a background hum of human conversation in his head. But in the early morning he is shaken by a dream. He's in a car driving at dusk along a fast country road, carefree and relaxed. Towards him comes a yellow VW Beetle. It's veering crazily across the road but he feels that he can avoid it, he's in control and at ease. But now it's on his side of the road and they are going to crash head-on. Just before impact he can see a woman's face behind the windscreen of the Beetle, her eyes round with surprise and fear. He wakes before the crash, shocked by the image of her, frightened, but relieved. It didn't happen. So he sleeps and dreams again. It is after the accident, he is in a hospital ward and at her bedside. She is pale, her dark hair framing her face and spreading onto the pillow, and she looks very small and vulnerable. One thin arm rests on the sheets attached to a drip. Everything around is clean and orderly. There are no other patients. At the end of the ward a large window looks out over the town and the sea beyond. He sits by the bed and holds her hand for a while but she doesn't return his grip and her face is still, without emotion. They don't speak. He awakes again and this time he's deeply disturbed. Strangely it is the second dream, in which nothing happens, that is difficult to erase from his mind.

It's morning now and he can hear the noise of traffic on the road outside. He's in an appallingly tasteless bedroom with cheap framed prints hung on pastel walls. The furniture pretends to be made from wood. There is a pink thick-pile carpet and the yellow bed-cover matches the curtains. Last night he was in a pub talking animatedly to people he will never meet again and now he's in an anonymous kitsch bedroom listening to traffic noise. He has just seen someone he loves lying injured in a hospital bed. What exactly is real? The question runs through his mind as he gets dressed for breakfast. What are the characteristics that make some things more real than others? Perhaps it doesn't matter. He puts the question out of his mind.

Rowing out to the boat again in the morning sunshine a single word catches his eye. On the stern of a large expensive yacht is the name of the place where it was registered. This is strange and it has happened to him many times before over the course of the last few years. Any mention of this particular city jars him and he meticulously shuts from his mind the memories attached to it. Why is that? Why is this one place and the time spent there so difficult for him? Was it more wonderful or more awful than the times they spent together along this coast? It's only natural that the importance of that period in his life should have diminished after all these years. Sailing this stretch of coastline has brought up memories – okay. He can put them to rest when he gets home again and gets on with real life. But perhaps there is some value to all this. Maybe he should lift the mental shutters from some more of this stuff and look at the time when they were most completely together, far from home, in a city where there was nobody who they knew or who knew them. For years he has had mental pictures of that city drifting into his mind from time to time, unexpectedly, and without reason. Just an image of a street scene, a park, or the docks. Often only that, a memory of a place. At other times he would find it more painful; the feeling of the two of them together there, the sense of her by his side.

They are outside a café by the city docks, sitting at one of the picnic tables that have been put there so that people can eat their lunch in the sunshine. It's not particularly sunny today but they can enjoy the view. They've finished their greasy food and are drinking tea from mugs. She lights a cigarette.

"I didn't think we'd be sitting looking out across water," he says. "It's what we always do but here it's so different. It's all straight lines, everything covered over with buildings."

"The water is different too," she says. "It's dirty and still."

"But you like it here don't you? Aren't you glad we came?"

"Yes, I like it a lot. I forget how stimulating the city is. So much going on. I love all the cranes and warehouses – makes me want to reach for my camera." She gives him a wicked teasing grin. "Yes I'd really like to come back alone and spend some days taking pictures. It would be brilliant."

"Right now I can't think of being here alone. I'd be expecting to see you around every corner."

She is looking at the water. A brightly-coloured ferry passes by, full of people, a dog standing on the bow sniffing the air happily. The docks lie along the course of what was once tidal river, so while the water is edged with cut stone and surrounded by buildings it still curves with the S shape of its original course. From where they sit they see the water bending round between large buildings and low hills covered in terraced houses. In one direction a tall church spire stands out above the industrial buildings.

"Why is it called the floating harbour?" she asks. "It's not floating."

"No, but the boats are. And they wouldn't be if the tide was allowed to come in and out naturally. Seems like a good name to me. Have you seen the top of those cranes? There's a cormorant at the very top of each one. Don't they look odd so far from the sea?"

They walk along the harbour-side looking down onto yachts and houseboats. From a building nearby comes the sound of someone playing a saxophone. A man on a jetty sends a tiny remote-controlled boat out across the oily water. Businessmen walk past boat-builders unloading welding equipment. Sometimes the sun comes out from behind the clouds and illuminates some of the city buildings.

"The best thing about you is how slowly you walk," she says.

He looks surprised, "But there's so much to see."

"That's what I think too but I've never found anyone before who can walk as slowly as me – and then stand still for ages."

"And then sit down," he says, matching words with action, or at least inaction.

They watch a man lifting a small child out of a pushchair to let him climb on a huge ship's anchor.

"Do you think that might suit me one day?" he asks.

"The stripy trousers or the ponytail?" she asks. "Neither of them. No way, not if you want to be with me."

"No, the other thing. You know, fatherhood."

There is a long pause.

"Same answer," she says, "don't even think about it."

They come to a dry dock, a finger of the harbour sealed off and pumped dry. A large wooden sailing ship is propped up inside awaiting repair. Unable to see properly, they climb the fence that's meant to keep people out. She walks along the harbour-edge and looks down on the vessel. She's fascinated by the shapes and patterns of masts and rigging, the curve of the ship's hull in the rectangle of the dock. She sits down on an old iron bollard and looks up at him.

"I've got a plan for taking some pictures. I'm sort of taking mental notes of where I'll come back to with a camera. I need to be alone for a few hours on the last day here. That's why I can leave my camera for now and concentrate on you. Okay?"

She looks at him with a mixture of assertiveness and pleading.

"But this is our first big trip together." He's immediately upset but tries to turn his mind around. "No, it's fine. I understand. I wish you'd said earlier that's all." He smiles but he can't completely hide the beginnings of disappointment that he feels. He knows he's being stupid.

"I need to see it from below," she says, and he has to follow her down the metal ladder to the bottom of the dock. They wander about in the strange space between the curved wooden side of the ship and the square granite blocks of the dock walls. The floor underneath them is concrete but covered in places with a film of sticky mud. There are odd piles of driftwood, leaves and pieces of rusty metal swept together in corners. They go up to the huge metal doors that hold back the water. He's aware of the mass of it there, outside, pressing to come in. Looking up at the sky framed by the walls of the dock he has an uncomfortable sense of being below sea level. The sky is very grey, there have been hints of rain during the afternoon and it has begun to get darker. Now the air cools, the wind picks up and a heavy rain begins to fall. There is only one place to take cover. They stand together, two small figures in the space of the dock, incongruous there, sheltering from the rain, keeping dry under a ship. They rub against each other to keep warm.

"This is surreal," he says, "the sort of thing that can only happen with a lover."

In the evening they are in something that feels like a nightclub in a cellar. It's actually on a boat, an old freighter converted into a venue for bands, moored in a wide part of the floating harbour. They are frisked on the way in by two bouncers in what appear to be chauffeur's uniforms. It's a spoof and turns into an improvised comic sketch. The city at night is a place of amiable irony. Nothing is what it seems. It doesn't matter. Everyone is your friend.

The evening starts with cabaret. Local comedians, including the chauffeurs, are mercilessly heckled by an audience that seems to made up of people they know. A lewd singer-songwriter encourages audience participation that culminates, in his last song, in a massed chorus of fake simultaneous orgasm and laughter. All the time she looks beautiful. She has tied her hair up into a dark fountain and wears a weird concoction of brightly coloured layers.

They are standing at the bar when the band comes on – five guys: electric guitar, bass, keyboard, drums, and vocalist. The music is punky and danceable and multi-textured. She is moving straight away. It's like a deep instinct in her, a sensual response to the rhythm. She's hedonistic and seductive tonight and much of his pleasure is in watching her.

They dance to a couple of numbers, bumping good-naturedly into others on the crowded floor. The music bounces off the inside of the vessel and rolls around them. It's pretty dark apart from the coloured spotlights on the stage and a few random beams of light on the dancers. Everyone is moving in rhythm. They stop for a while, she wants more to drink and also buys cigarettes. Then they dance again and he enjoys the sensation of watching others as he moves, spinning slowly around, his eyes always coming back to her. In an interval he goes to the toilet and when he returns she's talking to the band. She looks radiantly happy, animated, asking questions. She talks to the keyboard player, a young man with cropped blond hair, dungarees, and a string of beads. He's pointing at the keyboard and explaining something. She leans forward to his ear to be heard above the noise. Eventually she touches him on the arm and moves away, making her way back across the floor.

"No mixing desk," she says when she arrives back, "it's a great sound though – I can't believe they can do that. Only they need a better bass player – did you hear when he played the melody line? Nobody does that. Maybe he's about to leave and I could join the band! They need me."

He smiles but feels left out. "*I* need you," he says.

"I know, I know, I'm just fantasising. Are you going to dance or stand there looking solemn?" The band starts up again and the room starts moving.

Downstream of the harbour, the tide makes its way in and out through a deep gorge crossed by a suspension bridge. On a grassy slope at the side of the gorge, above the bridge and looking out over the city, is the little stone tower that holds the camera obscura. Inside on the top floor they are looking at an image of the world outside, projected down from a mirror in the ceiling. With other visitors they stand in a circle in the darkened room, around a wide white dish on which the moving images appear. A wooden arm moves the device in the roof and the circle of people pass it from hand to hand to move the picture. They can see people sitting on the grass, children running and playing, cars on the road, and a crow taking bread out of a bin. All the world outside, in fact, but upside-down to some of the people in the circle, and also without sound, a live silent movie. The pictures in front of them are only slightly different from what they could see if they stepped outside. But there's a nice unreality to the situation. A circle of people in the dark, as if at a séance, looking at a silent world that might be the past, the present or the future. He becomes absorbed in looking into this other dimension and doesn't notice that she has slipped away. In front of him is the projected image of people moving about on the grass below. A slender woman with dark hair crosses the scene. He turns and realises that she has gone out without him noticing. He loves to watch her from here but it feels unreal – as if looking back in time, like looking at old photographs. She sits down on the grass. Then she turns as if sensing that she is being watched. She looks coolly back at the tower. And then, remembering who is in there, she smiles and waves. He smiles at her image and wants to wave back. He goes down the wooden steps and out into the sunshine, relieved to see her for real. He sits on the grass beside her and they kiss. Then they look over their shoulders at the camera obscura watching them. They laugh and walk away.

"Seeing you through that thing," he says, "it reminds me of before we were together. If you came into a crowded room I would instantly know you were there. I would spot your figure on the street from miles away – not because I was consciously looking for you but because something in me was somehow responding to your presence."

She takes his hand as they walk, "But you never hinted to me or made a pass. I don't understand."

He looks at her lovingly, "I didn't think I had a chance. You were so talented and beautiful. Completely out of my reach. So I didn't allow myself to think of you in that way. Before I knew you I saw you once in that band. You were playing at the pub on the pier."

"Oh my God. We were awful. You never told me you'd seen us play."

"Well it was long before we were both in the mediaeval music group. I sort of forgot about it in a way. I mean it's true the band were awful. But you were on a stage – you were already on a pedestal."

She shakes her head, "I don't understand. I thought you didn't like me then. You hardly spoke to me."

He smiles, "I didn't know what to say."

They are at the edge of the gorge. Way below them it's high tide and sea water floods up towards the floating harbour.

"I knew there was something when we played music together," she says. "It's weird that you think of me as talented when you can play like that."

"You never gave me any indication either. Why was that?"

"I was so determined not to get involved again. To be me for a while."

"So what changed?"

She turns him towards her and kisses him.

"I couldn't resist you," she smiles, "and anyway, I thought you might be sane."

They walk onto the suspension bridge, and a strong wind blows up from the west and pushes her hair into disarray. Leaning on the parapet, they look down into the dirty water for a long time. Below them pieces of driftwood and rubbish are being carried into the city by the incoming tide. There's nobody else around. She pushes her hair down inside her jumper and looks at him very seriously.

"I'm going to tell you two things. No, three things. It's because I care for you that I'm telling you this stuff; it's not for anyone else to know. Also, we're not going to talk about this again, okay? First: I'm not having children. I've been a mother before, or at least I've been obliged to play that role. It took too much away from me – it took my creativity. So that's not going to happen again. Second: I can't believe this but it's true. I was once married. The guy was possessive, jealous, bullying really. It was so deeply crap for me, like I was wearing a strait-jacket or something. No one does that to me again. Third: there have been times when I've thought of suicide. I don't know why I'm telling you this but I guess it's all connected."

He doesn't know what to say. He can't understand it all at once. He doesn't know if her should touch her.

"Oh yeah, there's a fourth thing, so you're lucky. Want to know what it is?"

He nods.

"I love you."

She has made a list of all the places where she will take photographs and sets off now leaving him in a bookshop. They will meet at five in an art gallery café. He goes into the park on the hill and pays to go into a tower that gives a view over the city. He spends a long time at the top looking at the rooftops and the distant hills. He finds it odd without her by his side but he likes knowing that she is somewhere in the city and that they will see each other in a few hours. He loves her completely now. He loves her more than he has ever loved anyone else. The things that he couldn't cope with before, her anger, the times she seems selfish, the times she drinks too much, these things are part of who she is. As much a part of her as her beauty, the speed of her thoughts, her creativity, the way she moves. And the way she makes love.

He doesn't know what to buy her as a souvenir. Jewellery is dodgy. An art book is taking a chance. He wanders around and ends up buying a book for himself, a history of the floating harbour, full of old photographs of the places they have been together, with tall-masted ships and steam engines. He has gravitated to the bottom of the town, to the floating harbour. He waits to cross the water on a little swing bridge that has opened to allow a yacht to pass through. A crowd of people stand there waiting for the bridge to return to its normal position. An electric bell rings loudly till the bridge has stopped moving. Between the bodies of the other people he can see across to the big cranes, the ones that had cormorants on top. The birds have gone today but there's a woman with a camera on the dockside below. He can actually feel his face changing shape into a smile as he watches. But she has to get on with her photography of course. What should he do? He decides to stay on his side of the water and watch her.

She is taking photographs of the cranes. She's smiling and she waves as if to ask someone to move out of the way. Then she disappears behind a crane. He walks up and down looking across the water, waiting to get a sight of her again. She reappears and walks slowly along the water's edge, someone at her side. They both turn towards the water and he has to look away. But he saw that she is with someone he recognises, the keyboard player from the band, the one with the cropped blond hair. A strange thing happens. The band had done a slower number, a very catchy romantic rock ballad. A memorable song, the sort of thing that would stay in the mind of a lover and be associated forever after with a time, a place, and the person he loved. This song runs through his head now, as clear as the background music in a movie, full of romantic connotations. But he looks across the water and there she is, walking casually, laughing with the young guy from the band. He doesn't understand what's going on. He knows that he feels terrible.

Now he walks along his side of the water parallel to them, only glancing across occasionally. Each sight of them is a physical hurt to him. He knows that he will have to keep watching and waiting to find out what she's doing – the woman he loves, who so much wanted to spend the afternoon alone.

The young man points to a small old warehouse that has a colourful mural painted on the wall. They walk towards it, open the door and go in. The door shuts and he is left on his side of the water, unable to take his eyes off the door. But he can't stare at a door forever. Eventually he walks away into town, rambles about in a trance for a while before turning up at the art gallery forty minutes late.

She is sitting in the café with an empty coffee cup in front of her. She looks very angry.

"I stopped what I was doing and got a taxi here to be in time for you and I've waited and waited. Why?"

He can barely speak. He doesn't apologise but sits down across the table from her.

"Have you had a good time?" he asks.

"Yes, very good. A good time cut short to make sure I didn't keep you waiting. Do you have anything to say?"

"I'm sorry I was late," he says limply. "Have you taken lots of good pictures?" He is staring at her and she doesn't know why.

"Yes. Well no, not lots. I bumped into a guy from that band. A really nice man, the little one with the blond hair – you know, the keyboard player."

"Did you have a chat about their music?" he asks. He's trying to sound casual but he's still looking strange and she looks at him intently.

"Yes. But I'm worried about you. Are you alright?"

"What else did you do?" he says.

"I took photographs."

"Outside photographs?"

"Yes, of cranes. Look I don't understand what's going on here. What's wrong with you?"

"And you had a good afternoon?"

"Yes, yes, yes. Why are you looking so morbid?"

"In a warehouse with a mural on the wall?"

She is silent for a moment. Very surprised by what she is hearing, not understanding. "Yes, I went in the warehouse that the guys practise in. It was all by chance. But how do you know that?"

He doesn't answer and she's very concerned.

"How do you know about the warehouse? Look, I think I see what this is all about. You're jealous because I talked to a man that I met when you weren't there – actually a man who reminds me very much of my brother. But how did you know?"

"I was watching. I watched you from across the water. I'm sorry."

There is a long silence. He's never seen her so angry. As if she could hit him. Her eyes look very hard and her body is tense. She looks away from him, out of the window towards the harbour. She speaks without turning towards him, managing to make a joke though her voice is bitter.

"Come in Mission Control, can you hear me? We have a serious malfunction. Request permission to return to Planet Earth."

FIVE

Julian is lending his neighbours the little grey tractor, together with a tractor-driver in the shape of me. I've driven it before but he goes over some of its idiosyncrasies before I set out. I will be turning hay and it's perfect weather, sunshine predicted for a few days but also a breeze which apparently is just as important for drying the crop. I'm on the tractor, a cushion between me and the metal seat (it's going to be a long day) and a pack with food and drink and a notebook which I've taken to carrying everywhere with me these days.

The engine is ticking over and Julian has to raise his voice a little to be heard, "He really blows it, doesn't he? He loves her so much that he spends an afternoon buying a present for himself, spying on her, and then is late for their rendezvous. I think I've met a few guys like that." He has a self-satisfied smile on his face. He slowly moves his eyes away from me and looks at the cloudless sky, "I think it's going to be fine all day," he says. I think he has a problem separating fiction from reality.

When I reach the Cranbournes' farm Gareth is waiting, he's seen me driving up the lane. We attach a tedder to the back of the tractor. It consists of two wheels of metal spines that will rotate under power from the tractor and spread the wilting grass to dry in the sun and wind. We drive down to the field together and I'm given some instruction. The crop has been spread once and has partly dried to a pale green and fawn colour. Gareth shows me that the grass at the bottom is still green and damp. My tractor-work will turn the crop over and bring this damper grass up into the air and sunlight. Tomorrow it will be pushed into rows and baled for winter fodder. I will spend the day driving up and down this 23 acres.

I sometimes get the impression that farmers around here have lost the power of speech. Gareth isn't like that. He's a stocky powerfully-built man and he speaks only when it's necessary. But there's also a kindness and patience about his manner. Now he's walking around the tractor, checking it over. His face is lined and worn from working outdoors and maybe from more than that. I think he has been through some hardship in his life and in the end it has brought out a kindness in him, an ability to sympathise with others.

"Be careful when you turn," he says. "Remember there's a machine sticking out the back. There's nothing more embarrassing than driving across a field and realising that you're towing a length of the neighbour's fence behind you." He lets out a chuckle, "It happened to me once." He pats the side of the tractor as if it's one of his dogs, then turns and walks out of the field and back towards the farm.

The field I'm working in is a large oblong surrounded by big overgrown hedgerows scattered with mature oak and ash trees. The crop of hay is spread uniformly over this enclosed space. I have to concentrate on keeping my passes through the crop spaced out so that I don't miss any or overlap and waste my time. And, of course, I have to be careful when turning. Still it's easy. After the first twenty minutes or so I can look up from time to time and enjoy my surroundings. The surrounding trees give the field the look of a woodland clearing. There's an amazing variety of colour and shape; the foliage of each tree creates a different texture, changing in the breeze. The sky is a pale blue with occasional towering white clouds. The tractor is very small and the noise of the engine is soothing and mesmeric. There is no cab, I'm in the open air with the sun already warm enough for me to take off my jumper and T-shirt and just wear shorts. I drive up and down the field, half-aware of the scent of the drying hay and the breeze on my face and shoulders. For an accomplished daydreamer, like me, this is not work. My slow passage across the field is a sensual meditation. I have a feeling of calm, of mental stillness. Gradually this gives way to reverie – places, people, and snatches of conversation drifting into my mind. Sometimes I stop at the edge of the field and write a few sentences in my notebook.

He has decided to return to his home harbour. It will take several days to cover the short distance down the coast but it feels right to be heading back. There's no wind and he must use the diesel engine, but that's pleasant in its way. Perhaps today the noise will bring dolphins to play around the boat. Certainly the sound and the simple act of steering are a sort of meditation. A stilling of the mind. There's a summer haze today and he can't see far. He stares lazily ahead. But now there is a shape out there becoming clearer as he approaches. He throttles down. Something is floating on the water, resting on the surface as if weightless. It has a curious shape, like a long rock. It doesn't seem entirely inanimate. As he gets closer the haze thins to show a seal, motionless, not swimming, lying on top of the water. It is like an absurd apparition. He has a sudden realisation, steers hard to starboard and heads further out to sea. A while later he goes below and looks at the charts and the depth-sounder. Later still he can turn and continue his course southwards, parallel to the coast. He is bemused by what he has seen. The sea is extraordinary.

The cry of a gull passing overhead wakes him and he raises himself. He has been lying with his head on her thigh and as soon as he stirs she wakes too. She looks across at him, her eyes round as if with amazement, startled afresh with her feelings for him. They are transformed by each other's presence. Calmed. Enriched. By stepping through the brambles they have come to a sequestered spot, a rabbit-grazed lawn on the edge of the cliff, hidden from passers-by. The sea glimmers far below. They have kicked off their shoes and lie half-clothed in the sun. Another gull passes along the cliff edge and turns its head to look at them.

There is such a haze today that all demarcation between land and sea and air is lost in the near distance. There seems no solidity in their surroundings. Just a small green platform suspended above a shining sea. As they look out over what could be air or water or maybe some other even less substantial medium they can see below them one long straight line stretching out into the haze. She has no idea what it could be.

"It's a sarn," he says. "There are two or three of them in the bay, long straight lines of boulders stretching out to sea, just under the water. I think they're roads to Atlantis but people say they're something to do with glaciers. They're dangerous to boats at low water, you can run aground miles from the shore. Or see just a rock jutting from the sea miles from anywhere. Seals rest on them sometimes. It's strange that this thing that's underwater stands out clearly when everything else is so obscure."

She changes the subject. "You had your head on my lap," she says. "I think you did or maybe it isn't a lap when I'm lying down. It sort of comes and goes."

It's a time and place where two people can exchange vague nonsense; half listening, half understanding, the companionable absurdities of lovers.

"But if you were standing," he says, "and my head was there, it would seem quite different."

She smiles, "I would wonder about your intentions."

He lies on his back beside her in the sunshine.

"Sometimes it seems the centre of all your sensation, all your pleasure."

"What does?" she asks.

"You know, your lap. Or thereabouts." He looks up at her silhouette against the hazy blue.

"Now that you mention it," she says, and looks at him with an enthusiastic smile, running her hand over his bare chest to his stomach.

"Before we became lovers," he says, "I thought of how we would be together. I only thought of it once. Honestly. And I thought it would be very delicate and tender. Lots of subtle slow arousal. Exploring each other's bodies over time."

She kisses him on his stomach just above his navel. She nibbles at his warm brown skin and makes a wet mark with her tongue.

"But the truth is," he continues, "mostly we just screw. For hours."

She sits astride him, holds his hands above his head and kisses the side of his neck. "We do," she says, rubbing herself against him. "That's what we do," and she lets out a sigh of happy resignation.

"Again and again," he says, "more than ever with anyone else."

"Again and again," she repeats. "Do stop talking."

I stop the tractor and walk to the top of the field to sit down with my lunch. Now, without the engine-noise, my daydreams subside; when I've finished eating, I gradually become more aware of my surroundings. I notice the small alternation of sunlight and shade in the leaves of the hedgerow nearby. The same pattern of light and dark is repeated on the trees running down along the edge of the field, and on the hills in the distance, marked by the shadows of clouds. It is a dappled land. More than this – everything is in motion. The breeze moves individual leaves back and forth in and out of sunlight, it pushes gently against the feathery branches of trees, moving them to and fro. The underside of some leaves show silvery grey in the wind and then subside to green again. Nearby, brown butterflies flicker along the edge of the bushes. A small bird bends a twig with its weight.

There's a sweet smell of hay. But it's more than that – it smells of warmth, of the sunshine itself. There's nowhere else I would rather be; nothing I would rather do than lose myself in these sensations. The sounds change as the breeze picks up and subsides again: first wind in the trees, then the nearer buzz of insects. I realise that the light is unusually clear today. I can see a long way very easily. But it's not a sharp light, there's just a little softness about it. Perhaps it's because the sky is now half full of white clouds or maybe it's the air itself, clear but softened with a little moisture. It is this quality of light that seems to give everything such beauty. The most ephemeral and intangible quality of my surroundings is the one that matters most.

Later I'm back on the tractor with the repetitive sound of the diesel engine setting a rhythm for my thoughts, making slow progress southwards along the coast and hoping to see dolphins. I can hear a voice above the engine noise and I throttle down.

"John, I've brought you a flask of tea," says Olivia. "Wow, were you in a daydream. I thought I'd have to lie down in front of the tractor to get your attention." I disconnect the power to the tedder and stop the engine. "Daydreaming's what I'm good at," I say. "And look at how much of the hay I've done."

It's mid-afternoon and I've turned most of the big field. The sun is behind clouds now and I look for the jumper that was on the back of my seat earlier in the day.

"Have you lost something?" she asks.

"My jumper, I think it's fallen off. It's here somewhere," I say, looking out across the field. She starts walking through the hay looking for it. "When did you lose it?" she asks.

"Sometime today."

"What colour is it?"

"A sort of fawn green," I say, picking up a handful of hay, suddenly feeling rather foolish. "Something like this."

"It'll turn up in the winter when we feed the cattle," Olivia says, trying not to laugh. "I'll make sure it gets back to you but it might be unwearable."

We sit down at the edge of the field to drink the tea. We talk about the weather and about farm life. Then she surprises me, "Julian tells me you're writing a novel," she says.

"I don't think it will amount to a novel. It's just a story. It's a silly self-indulgent thing to do. But it's a cheap hobby."

"I think that Julian believes it to be very good. Or at least it affects him a great deal. But he won't tell me what it's about."

"It's about a love affair. The best thing ever. That went wrong."

She has caught me at a funny time. I can't decide whether I want to talk a lot or not at all.

"It sounds as if it might be autobiographical," she says.

Olivia is a nice woman. Different from the strong, tough personality that I see when she's with others. Today she empathises a great deal, her face picking up my feelings and reflecting them back to me. I want her to ask more but I know that she probably won't.

"Perhaps it is autobiographical," I say. "It's changed and distorted but maybe somewhere, in its essence, it is about me."

"So no wonder you and Julian are close. You must talk about these things a lot when you're working together."

"Yes and no. There's plenty of reserve. There's so much we don't say. I know very little about what he's up to these days." I pause and she's about to speak, maybe to talk about Julian and his present relationship. I get in first, "But actually I don't want to know."

She must have heard the panic in my voice and now she looks at me carefully. Her brows are pushed together in puzzlement. I feel the need to get back on the tractor but I haven't finished my tea. I think she senses my difficulty but she pushes on regardless.

"Isn't it difficult disinterring old relationships?" she asks.

"It was a very long time ago. And I'm fictionalising it, changing it. That puts a distance between me and the reality of what happened."

"Ah, reality. I seem to remember Julian telling me that you're not so keen on the idea of reality." She teases me now, her eyes sparkling with mischief. "I think you're admitting its existence."

I know I didn't mean reality. I know that what I'm succeeding in distancing myself from is something else. But she looks like she's scored a point so I have to put her straight.

"Actually it's something very different from reality that I'm able to keep at bay. It's feelings. All the emotions I once had about that affair, they're old now, played out. I can step back from them."

"It doesn't sound like a very good novel then."

"But you've just said that Julian likes it," I respond.

This is a strange conversation. Partly we're sparring. Trying to prove each other wrong. Also I'm talking about things I didn't expect to talk about today, least of all with Olivia.

"It affects Julian," she says, "I think it holds up something to which he can compare his current relationship. And it reinforces some of his perceptions of her."

I find I'm looking very intently at the cup of tea that I'm holding. There is one particular word I really don't want to hear. A woman's name. When I look up I can see that Olivia is surprised by the look on my face. She sounds concerned, "You look like you've seen a ghost." I manage a limp smile. I can't explain.

"Perhaps we should talk about something else," she says.

There's a long silence between us. I'm aware of the sound of the wind in the trees. I guess she thinks it's strange that I don't want to know anything about Julian's present relationship. And she wonders why my story has an emotional effect on him.

"How long ago was it?" she asks, "the old love affair in the story?"

"It's about something that happened many, many years ago. A really long time." I know the exact date on which it ended. I know how many years and months it has been but I don't say.

"And this woman – you don't keep in contact?"

"No."

"Why not? Couldn't you be friends?"

"No. Lovers or nothing. Actually if we saw each other we would either love each other or hate each other. Both probably."

Olivia smiles, "What if she knew that you were writing a novel about her – I wonder what effect that would have on her."

"No. Julian would never tell her about it. I'm sure of that."

So Olivia knows. I think Julian and I are very carefully pretending that fiction is fiction. We're keeping the truth from each other and, to some extent, from ourselves. I wonder why he keeps reading and I guess that it's the same reason that anyone reads a story. You want to know what will happen next. And for some reason he wants to know more about her past. I guess I have some power over the guy, I can write whatever I want him to read and choose to alter his present perceptions with my fiction. I've always said that none of it is real. But Julian is my friend.

SIX

From the sea he sometimes catches sight of the little train that runs along the coast. It seems a tiny insignificant thing below the large mass of the hills. But it's the only thing moving and, in some places, the only sign of humanity on the bleak coastline. It passes along the bottom of cliffs, over vast empty salt-marshes and past tidal creeks. It clatters across a wide estuary on a wooden bridge. Sometimes it disappears into a tunnel and the sound it makes is switched off and then on again as it re-emerges. However, from a distance the sounds are unsynchronised, like a badly dubbed film. The train connects a number of small seaside towns. They are different from each other but share many of the same features, perhaps a castle, a small harbour with sailing boats, a beach and promenade. Houses spreading a little way up the hillside. Hotels and bed-and-breakfast establishments with large windows looking out to sea.

He wakes beside her and carefully, not disturbing her sleep, he pushes himself up the bed so his head is propped on the pillow and he can look sideways through the big window. He looks across a few rooftops and garden trees to the beach below and the waves coming in. Here the waves break in perfect long lines of turning water, the crests forming and collapsing at one end of the beach and running neatly down along the line of swell to the other. He watches for some time. There are two lines of movement: the waves advancing up the beach towards him, and the sideways run of each crest as it crosses his view from right to left. Further down the coast the waves are chaotic and ragged but here some particular configuration of headland and beach allows the surf to form this perfect regular pattern. The window is shut, he's watching the sea through glass and no sound reaches him. But he can't get up and open the window yet or he will wake her.

He turns his head now and looks at her, at the long strands of her almost-black hair on the pillow, and the softness of her face in sleep. He feels an overpowering tenderness towards her, an emotion that has some physical presence in his body. His breathing has slowed and deepened as if expressing the character of his feeling for her. Lying there with her beside him, both of them motionless in the silent room, he is intensely alive. He doesn't move. The only sound is of her breathing. How curious to feel in such stillness a vitality. He allows himself just a little sigh and she wakes. She opens her eyes, looking straight into his face. He touches her lips very gently with his. Then her shoulder, her collarbone, the side of her throat, her earlobe. He moves the sheet down a little and kisses the side of her breast. She stretches herself happily for him to express his love for her. He touches her very gently and tenderly. It is strange to him that in a little while they will be forcing themselves against each other almost aggressively. He knows it will be so, as it was before they slept last night. Strange that the most pure wordless expression of their love is, at its most intense, something she once described as vicious. And in his tenderness for her now, even as they both begin to feel the stronger urges, he can't quite believe that love is expressed in something that seems like anger. He is held back a little, both by his tenderness and by the part of him that muses on the act of love. She rolls him over onto his back, playfully, and then urgently, bringing the two of them together. And now no part of him muses. All of him is lost in this lovemaking. Ordinary consciousness departs and both of them are completely taken over by the giving and receiving of sensual pleasure.

They have finished or paused – they never know which. They move their bodies a little away from each other and he can see the alarm clock. It is only seven and they are very much awake. He moves around the room naked and makes tea. He opens the window to let in the sound of the distant surf. He brings two cups of tea and gets into bed beside her but she gets up and goes to sit in a chair by the open window. She lights a cigarette and sits there looking sensually fulfilled against the backdrop of the sea.

"Beautiful, beautiful, beautiful, beautiful," he says. It's what he feels. But he also feels that she's separated herself from him; and he doesn't like the smell of cigarette smoke so early in the day. He can't mention it: she would hear the irritation in his voice and it would spoil their perfect morning. This is a problem for him. They are so wonderful together but, being human beings, their love has flaws. Things that for each other take away the perfection of the moment. He feels that he loves her completely for every-thing that she is. But that's not the whole truth: part of him is angry with her for not being all he wants her to be. He hides this from himself. Propped up on the bed with his tea in one hand he can see his reflection in the mirror of the dressing table. His face has softened with the catharsis of love-making. But he's surprised to see in his eyes something other than the intense happiness that he knows was there earlier. He is with the woman he has loved most of all in his life. He believes that she feels the same for him, and the two of them express their feelings often and with great passion. So how can this be? He looks at his face in the mirror and sees something like disappointment.

They are on a grassy bank below the castle wall, beyond their feet the land drops quickly down to the rocks at the edge of the sea. The day has turned out sunny with summer haze in the distance and a golden pellucid light on the grass and rough stone walls of the castle. The sea that can so often be grey and murky in the bay is today as it should be – a vibrant blue. Below the lovers, on the deep clear water that surrounds the castle mound, there is a sailing boat. It has all sails set to catch the small breeze, and their white curves stand out against the blue. It seems to be a large vessel to have only one person on board – a stocky man, standing at the wheel, concentrating on picking up the wind and getting away from the noise of the town. Looking down from above there's a romance about this figure, a sense of purpose.

"Someday that's me," he says, "when I'm rich and middle-aged, with no ties."

"When exactly does middle age start?" she asks him provocatively. "And when do you get rich?" she says, "I'm really interested in that."

They are carefree, joking, so it surprises him that he comes out with the answer he does: "I get middle-aged when we go our separate ways. I think I'll age quite suddenly, like something out of a science-fiction film. I'll look in the mirror and suddenly see an aged face staring back at me."

"And you'll go sailing?"

"When I've recovered. I can't imagine recovering but I will and I'll be rich, goodness knows how, and turn my eyes to the sea and sail away from all my earthly troubles."

He is smiling still. Standing there on the promontory, looking out over the sea with her beside him, he can't really imagine that his future might hold loneliness.

"You know things are different from how they seem," she says. "Maybe sailing isn't much fun, it just looks like that from the distance. Things aren't the same on the inside as they are viewed from afar."

"Like being in love," he says. "It probably seems ridiculous to everyone else."

"Or like being drunk," she says, "all your cares blown out of the window but you look really stupid."

He doesn't seem to have heard this. He is still looking at the sea and at the sailing boat pulling out away from the land but he's thinking of something else.

"When we were in the bath together last night," he says, "I felt like making a solemn vow. A daft one but it seemed right. I thought there's no one else in the world I would want to be with like this. And it felt that I would always think that. I wanted to promise that I will never, in all my life, get into a bath with another woman."

"Or man?" she asks.

"Or man. Actually I don't think I'm that way inclined."

"You don't really know. Have you ever tried it?"

"No," he smiles.

"Well, you don't know then."

He has to think about this. "I think I do know," he says. "First there's you. You are at the centre of my emotional, romantic, sexual feelings. Without you? I can't imagine it. But one day I suppose I would have some feelings for someone again. And it would be a woman not a man. It's in my nature. It's who I am."

She is looking at him carefully. She doesn't want to accept this.

"I think you underestimate the power of culture," she says. "You get conditioned. Imagine if you were brought up in a culture where homosexuality was the norm."

"I like this part of us together – the intellectual part."

"Are you changing the subject?"

"Yes, because I don't really know what to tell you. I'll think about it. How come you question all this stuff?"

"My brother is bisexual. We've talked about it a lot."

But he wants to leave this subject.

"Can we get back to the bath?" he says. "There was something I was building up to. I wanted to tell you that you're my eternal bathmate. How does it feel?"

She lifts his hand off the grass and holds it between her own.

"Wet?" she says, and laughs.

Later the afternoon is turning cool and dull with clouds and a cold wind arriving from the west. The sea is grey and is beginning to form into small waves that beat against the rocks below the castle. They have walked up through the town to the station and have caught the little train that runs around the bay. They've been on it a few times since the accident that left her unwilling to travel by car. The journey is slow and scenic and might be perfect for lovers but the windows of the train are very dirty and this intensifies the growing dullness. She is drinking the first of two cans of lager that she bought for the train ride and he sits opposite her with a small carton of orange juice as if in defiance.

"I worry about how much you drink and smoke nowadays," he says, knowing it's probably a mistake.

"You don't worry, you disapprove. Okay, disapprove but be honest about it. Either way it makes no difference. I don't conform to your or anyone else's petty hair-shirt parsimony."

He laughs. "Isn't that a flower? *The petty hairshirt parsimony.* Sounds like it grows in church walls."

But she won't smile. Anything that seems like a criticism will always arouse anger in her. And now he feels touchy too.

"If I say the wrong thing you're angry," he says.

"I'm not angry," she replies with unconvincing calmness. But he won't leave it now. "What it means," he says, "is that there are subjects that I can never touch on. Things that we can never speak about reasonably and come to some understanding."

"What you call understanding is me being who you want me to be. Men do that *so* much. It's never, 'I love you, what can I do to make you happy?' but, 'I love you, wash the dishes; I love you, do what I say." And now she is angry.

"I only want us to be able to talk. That's all."

Normally he loves the rhythm of the train and the gradually-changing views of the coast. But he has become irritable and looks moodily out of the window at the dirty sheep grazing the salt-marshes. It's a Bank Holiday tomorrow; they could have spent the day together, but she has other plans.

"I'm going to Mark's house for the day," she says. "He has a new graphics programme that does things to photographs. It's really cool. I'm very lucky to have someone who can teach me how to use it."

"Oh, I thought it was work, that's what you said." His voice has a little barbed edge

"It *is* my work. I can't believe you're doing this. It's the most important thing to me. I believe I've said that before, you know it and you try to undermine me by criticising."

"I'm not criticising. I haven't said anything."

For her now the view out of the window is profoundly interesting and he finds himself looking across the carriage and out of the opposite window. Her voice had risen in pitch as she had spoken to him and now that irritating confrontational tone, the tone she adopts so quickly if he has said the wrong thing, rings around inside his head. He tries to look out through the dirty glass but has difficulty focussing on the bleak hillside beyond. Instead he can see a reflection of her, facing away from him, silhouetted against the background of the grey sky and sea.

He turns to her. "I suppose I'm old-fashioned," he says, "I think of work as involving being paid. Something a person might do to earn money. Something that a person might do to pay off their debts."

"Another way of getting at me. You always want to go up and down the coast to see some other bit of dreary seaside. You're keen to lend me more money and get some sort of hold on me. Well next time go alone. I've got better things to do."

The man opposite gets up and moves to a seat at the end of the carriage. The train has entered a short tunnel and its noise increases, forcing a pause in their speech. Then it emerges into the light again and passes along the foot of the cliffs, close to the breaking waves.

"Why are you on this train with me anyway?" she asks. "You could have stayed another day. Spent the day looking at stupid sailing boats."

He doesn't answer and she asks again, "Why are you here on this train with me if everything I do is so wrong?"

This is her favoured form of attack – the confrontational rhetorical question. He has learnt not to answer; he knows that any attempt at rational argument is futile. There is a long pause. The train has stopped at a tiny station that doesn't seem to be near any human habitation. A woman with two young children has got on and passes to the end of the carriage away from them.

He's thinking of reconciliation now but doesn't know if he can make the effort. She has taken a second can of beer from her bag and opened it. He looks at her face hardened with anger.

The train is now pulling onto the long wooden viaduct that crosses the estuary here. It is high tide and they are surrounded by sea water as they clatter slowly across the bridge.

"How is Mark nowadays?" he asks. "Still as personable as ever?" He tries to stop himself but fails. "Better company than me anyway."

She turns from the window for long enough to speak. "Yes. Better."

"Then you ought to spend more fucking time with him."

He knows he's unreasonable and jealous. He knows it's the worst possible thing he can do in his relationship with her. She faces away from him still, looking through the grimy window at the sea. By the set of her shoulders he can see her mood. Then she looks towards him, her eyes narrowed in spite.

"More fucking time with him," she turns the words over carefully. "There's an idea. I know it's going to be a long day, just me and him. I'll tell him you suggested it."

She lifts her can of beer to her mouth and drinks, looking at him with a mixture of contempt and cold anger. He stands and walks down the carriage away from her. The automatic door closes behind him. He walks through the other two carriages to be as far away from her as he can. It doesn't feel far enough. The train stops. He opens the door and steps onto the platform.

He turns his back as the train pulls out, looking down at his feet as its noise diminishes with distance. Only when he can't hear it anymore does he look around him. He feels superficially calm and goes to the timetable on the wall and makes a mental note of the time of the next train. He has an hour and walks down to the sea. It's a bank holiday weekend and the promenade and beach are full of families. Children are making sand-castles and running in and out of the sea. People are playing cricket on the sand. There's a sound of laughter and of games and happy activity. This, to him, is profoundly incongruous. The sky has been clouded over for a while now and the air is chilly. It's a dull cool day by a grey sea. But the people he can see believe it to be something else. Perhaps it's because it's a bank holiday. Of course they are simply making the most of their short time at the seaside – they don't live near the sea like him. But as he watches them he feels that they see something that he can't. Theirs is a world of sunshine and happiness while his is one of grey gloom.

To get away from the worst of the crowds he sits down on a bench in a small park that stretches back away from the sea. There is now a gradual fall of drizzle, very soft and fine, barely wetting him. He is unable to tell whether there are still children playing on the beach or if they've taken shelter now. The only other person in the park is an old man walking a dog, making a slow circuit under the trees. As the man passes he looks across and says a word in such a way that it's impossible to guess if it's a question or a statement,

"Lonesome."

This word is a mirror held up to him. He can imagine what a huddled forlorn figure he makes in the empty park. There's something unreal and unlikely about this sudden descent. He manages a wan smile.

On the next train he tries to keep a level, unemotional state of mind. But what if one day something like this is the end of them? The thought tries to penetrate his calm. It is not to be contemplated. A dark free-fall.

The train pulls into his station and he gets off into near darkness and rain. He makes for a bench under the awning where he can sit and decide what to do. He thinks that he will get his car and drive to his house without attempting to see her tonight. That particular way of hurting him was savage. Too much to risk again. He looks along the platform at the rain falling on tarmac and concrete. Nearby is a telephone box, its fluorescent light coldly illuminating a dirty puddle. How could a single day contain so much contrast? Sunlight on clear blue sea to start with. And now this sense of alienation. Cold artificial light on rain water, dirt and concrete.

He gets up and walks towards the end of the platform and the exit. He is aware of the particular smell of the station. Of dust and wet railway sleepers. Only when he gets near the exit does he realise there's a figure standing in the dark watching him. She takes one step forward and holds out the bag that he left on the train. He takes it from her and they stand looking at each other. She is pale and motionless. When a gust of wind moves her hair a little he leans forward tentatively and touches her cheek with his lips. At that instant, without any transition from one state to another, she begins to cry uncontrollably like a distraught child. Her legs give way beneath her and she collapses into his arms. He has to help her to a bench, her thin body convulsing against him, her sobbing loud on the empty platform. It is some time before she will speak through a mixture of smiles and tears.

"I thought I was going into a dark tunnel. I mean that's how it felt to me. And then I really was. And it was so funny and pathetic that I wanted to tell someone about it. Who do I tell my stupid things to? Only you."

Julian stops the little grey tractor in the shade under an oak tree. Later, when he's finished cutting summer cabbages and lettuces, he will load his harvested crops onto the metal box at the back of the tractor and take them up to the farmyard. He passes where I'm crouched over, weeding a long bed of carrots.

"Why don't you give your lovers names?" he says. "I've never read a story where the characters don't have names."

"Well, that's how it is."

"It would make it more real."

"The trouble with you, Julian, is that you're too literal-minded."

"What do you mean by that?"

"You want it all wrapped up, straightforward, understood.

Nothing is ever really like that."

"I still think they should have names."

Julian is pushing me. I don't know why.

"Suggest some names," I say, feeling that I'm taking some sort of chance.

"The woman could be..." he pauses and looks me. "What about Catherine?"

"No."

"And the man is Sean. A nice name, Irish I believe."

"I don't think so."

I hope he will move on and leave me to work. He hangs around for a while and I begin to feel uncomfortable. Then he starts to go but turns to ask another question.

"How come you can spend your days with me when you know I'm seeing her?" he says.

"I don't know. I'll get back to you on that."

So we've started to talk about the unmentionable. It feels more honest than when we pretended that my story was entirely fiction. Julian doesn't know how much of it is about real things that happened between me and her all those years ago and, strangely enough, I'm not really very clear either. It's interesting. I think I'm okay with it.

He has walked to the bottom of the field with crates that he will fill with vegetables; using a sharp knife, he begins to cut the first cabbages. This is the work he likes the best. He looks fulfilled and moves with his characteristic grace and a sensual *joie de vivre*. I'm used to being around him and spending a lot of time with him without speaking, so I can tell his mood from his body-language. Now his movements are expansive. When he walks up the rows to get more crates his head is held high, he's happy and at ease with himself. As for me, I enjoy the sensual pleasure of sun on skin and warm soil under my bare feet. My surroundings are beautiful, here in the lower field the sun has brought out dragon-flies and, because it's the first hot sun after a period of rain, lots of newly-emerged brightly-coloured butterflies.

And now I'm trying to find the answer to his question – how *can* I spend my days with him when I know that he's seeing her? My fingers are moving fast among the young carrot plants, pulling out weeds and tossing them onto the path behind me. My mind moves more slowly. I realise that I get a strange buzz out of seeing Julian. I notice it when I haven't seen him for a few days and he phones to say the weather will be good and he has some work for me. I feel excited as if anticipating seeing a lover. It's because seeing him is a small safe link with her. I can feel some connection to her without any risk of touching real feelings. She never comes here, I know that. Also he hasn't told her that I'm working for him and I know he would never speak to her of my writing. And now, separated by the years from emotions, I can feel no jealousy. He is working closer to me now, cutting cabbages and putting them into crates, sometimes squashing caterpillars between his fingers when he finds them on his crop. He wears only shorts, boots and a stone pendant on a string around his neck. Did she give it to him? I take a little spiteful pleasure in noting that it doesn't look very good.

There's an area across the back of Julian's neck and shoulders that is so darkly tanned that it resembles the skin of a black man. Elsewhere he's just a warm golden colour. I occasionally glance up from my work and my eyes are drawn to this very dark skin. I imagine her fingers there. I know how it would be, her half-artist, half-lover fascination with the changing tones and textures of his body. I know where her fingers would go, and how she would touch him, and the look of almost reverence in her eyes as the tips of her fingers move down and across his body. Julian stands and straightens his back, picks up some full crates, and carries them to where he can pick them up with the tractor. The muscles of his arms and shoulders tense as he lifts them. For a moment I believe that I can see him through her eyes. For a briefer moment I want to touch him where she would touch him. Then he drives off with a full load on the back of the tractor and I stop my work, straighten up and walk along the hedgerow. I need to think about other things now.

It's high summer and the leaves of the hedgerow trees and bushes are dark against the lighter colours of grass and crops. Only the oaks have a little paler colour at the end of their branches where they've made a second burst of growth. I see that there are tiny hints of the next season already. Rowan berries have a tinge of orange to them. The first blackberries are nearly ripe and hazelnuts are swelling their pale green shells. Okay, so there's not the delicate beauty of spring but there is something special about the heat, the buzz of insects, and this new voluptuousness along the hedgerow.

I have finished weeding one bed of carrots and started the next when Julian comes back into the field and decides to work with me for a while before we stop for lunch.

"You don't have to answer my question," he says, "I just wonder if you feel any jealousy towards me. You certainly don't show any signs of it."

"No I don't. I went through all that. I don't need to feel that much emotion around this subject any more. I feel safe."

"Then why can't you two be friends? Why can't you see each other one day and it's alright?"

"I can't speak for her. Or maybe it's the same, I don't know. For me there's a lot of anger. We hurt each other very much. I caught a glimpse of her in her car last year. I felt so much anger. Hate maybe."

"You caught a glimpse of her in her car last year and you still remember it? I don't understand. And you don't ask me about her. If you loved her that much don't you want to know how she is now? She's been through some really tough times – things you can't imagine."

"I'm sorry."

We are silent as we walk up to the farm for lunch. Near the top of the next field he speaks, "I'd like to understand why you two can't even talk to each other."

I don't want to answer. I feel very agitated. As we walk into the farmyard he says something else. I'm trying not to hear but one word cuts into me. He says her name. And now this is all getting too real. We walk to the back of the barn and take off our few clothes to shower. When I'm under the cold water and Julian is standing in the sun drying himself with his T-shirt, he turns to me with a sympathetic smile.

"You still love her, don't you?"

I can't speak. I nod my head. The water runs through my hair, across my face and down on to the ground. I turn away from him. With some self-control I get partially dressed and we walk around the barn to the farmhouse. I sit in the sun looking across at the boat sticking out of the end of the barn and Julian goes inside to make tea. When he comes out I tell him that I don't feel very well. I don't like to let him down but I've got to go home. I pick up the bag that contains my untouched lunch, get into my car and drive away.

SEVEN

The wind will be force four, perhaps closer to force five later in the day, south-westerly. Good visibility, occasional showers, stronger winds and rain later in the week. This is good sailing weather for a man who wants to get down the coast and home in as few days as possible. Stronger winds than he has had on the trip so far – and they've come at the right time, as his confidence in single-handed sailing has grown. And today a clear light, sunshine, and occasional towering clouds. He leaves the harbour among other boats crewed by people making the most of this good weather. He has studied the chart for the bay over breakfast and also given some thought to the tides. He has a choice of two possible harbours down the coast that will be deep enough for him to get ashore in the early evening. He is excited about being on the sea and keen to be going home. He also feels the tiniest trepidation, something less than fear, something that combines with other feelings to increase his excitement this morning. To make some distance today he will sail close to the wind.

Speed, distance and time are all perceived differently on the sea. A speed like eight knots, which would seem slow on a bicycle going down a country lane, feels exhilarating and fast on a sailing boat pushing through the waves. Distances are great. You might be in clear sight of your destination – a small town further down the coast, for instance – but it will take three hours of good sailing to reach it, tacking back and forth across the wind. And it will be a long three hours, with only subtle changes in the wind and the sea. As for time, a day will be both long and short. Long as it slowly passes, short in retrospect, with an absence of events to remember it by. He remembers time being distorted in a different way again.

With her, many hours would go by without them being aware

of their passing. But looking back over a day or a week there would always be a feeling of a great deal having happened. Changes in their relationship filled their days with greatly contrasting emotions. From imminent loss and loneliness to extraordinary happiness and back again. From love and the expression of love to anger and spite. And always, in the little time available to assimilate all these changes, amazement that some seemingly distant memory of how they once were was actually the recollection of events which had happened just a few days ago.

He had valued this intense emotional activity for a while. The sense of being very much alive. Such pain and such pleasure. She had once told him of Eskimos always having to experience the pain of their frozen hands and feet warming up and coming back to life. But if they didn't hurt, well then you had frost-bite and were in danger of gangrene and death. So pain is good – it means you're alive. Curiously he had heard of the same sort of thing with the Bedouin in the desert. A celebration of pain as a sign of life continuing. Towards the end of their time together he had begun to have had enough of such pain. Enough of the continual hurt they inflicted on each other.

He has been tacking close in to the wind and heading out into the bay. Now he turns the boat, the wind fills the other side of the sails and he runs in towards and along the coast, the wind on the starboard beam now, the boat keeling-over to port. Closer to the shore he can gradually see more of the largest town in the bay. Like most seaside towns it looks better viewed from the sea. You can't see the railway sidings or gasworks but instead the long terraces of fine Victorian houses on the front and above them large handsome buildings looking out over the sea. The library. The university. Near to the top of the hill, the hospital.

He walks up flights of stairs to the top floor of the hospital, it doesn't occur to him to use the lift. As he climbs he becomes aware of more aches and pains in different parts of his body, particularly around his chest and shoulders. But he knows that he is only bruised. What hurts more is that the accident should have happened at all. He tries to make sense of it, a particular kind of sense that excuses his or her part in it and blames outward circumstances. He will wear a puzzled look on his face from time to time over the next few days, until he has sorted it out in his mind.

In the ward he is told by a nurse that he will find her in the end bed by the windows. There he sees a small figure outlined by a white sheet, bandages around her head, a drip attached to one arm and some sort of monitor wired to her. Worse than he thought. He feels himself tightening up inside and prepares himself for more. He walks slowly down the ward. Then he hears his name being called from the bed opposite.

"Sean," she says, "I'm here."

He turns and there she is, smiling at him. He is relieved, very happy to see her, and amused by his mistake. He goes to her bed and takes her hand. Despite the accident, the physical pain they are in, and the shock of what they have been through, they look at each other now with what is, in this place, an incongruous happiness. He puts his mouth close to her ear, "Catherine," he says, "I love you."

She smiles, "I'm stoned. It's the pain killers, they're great. And you look so good."

"What have they said? Are you going to be okay?"

"I've got lots of bruises, broken ribs. I'm probably alright inside but they want to do more scans and x-rays. I moaned so much in the night that they gave me these amazing pain-killers and I feel fine now. And seeing you, of course."

She is pale with a little dark under her eyes and she has an elaborate plaster on her forehead that she seems unaware of. To him she seems small and delicate in the large hospital bed. But she is genuinely carefree and relaxed, made so either by his presence or by the drugs. Her hair has been tied into two bunches either side of her head and is dark on the white pillow. He looks at her eyes and notices how large her pupils are. There is a new person for him to love here, someone fragile where before there was someone tough. He tells her that he nearly went to the wrong bed.

"How fickle men are," she says, teasing. She is smiling that strange smile where her lower lip arches down. He leans over and kisses her very carefully.

"That was nice," she says. "But it's all you'll be getting from me for a while."

For a few days Sean visits her in hospital. She is serenely happy when he is there for her and the nurses have taken to talking about them as if they are young lovers. They avoid talking about the accident. On the third day they are discussing bruises.

"I'll show you mine if you show me yours," she says with a coy smile.

He lifts his shirt to show his most spectacular bruise where he had been forced against the car's seat-belt. She looks at him with a humorous mock admiration.

"Will you draw the curtains?" she asks.

When they are shielded from the view of the other patients she eases the sheet down and carefully lifts her night-dress, wincing at the pain of her movements.

"I don't think you can compete with this," she says.

She has large, dark purple, almost black areas of bruising around one hip, across her ribs and on one arm. There are many other smaller bruises of lighter colours. In the few places where she hasn't been hurt he sees that her skin is unblemished and milky. It is a strangely tender act for her to reveal herself to him like this. The frankness of a lover showing all of who she is, nothing hidden. He looks for somewhere to place a kiss, a part of her that he won't hurt by touching. He places a chaste kiss on the top of one thigh.

She lets out a sigh, "It's going to be difficult for a while. Every movement hurts."

"It's alright."

"Will you kiss me here where the bruising is darkest?" she says, pointing to her hip. Some parts of her body seem lost under dark shadows. The most strongly-coloured area is over her ribs just below her breasts but he kisses the place she points to. He must be looking questioningly at her. After she has rearranged her night-dress and pulled up the sheet she says, "I don't know why."

He draws the curtains back and sits at her bedside again. They are quiet, almost solemn, but fulfilled by each other's presence. There are visitors coming and going to other patients on the ward and making unnecessary conversation with forced jollity. He looks out through the large window across the town to the sea, a uniform grey mass today, ending abruptly at a clear horizon and divided into irregular shapes by the larger buildings below the hospital.

She keeps very still and when her pain has eased a little she speaks with enthusiasm.

"Will you help me when I get out of here?" she says. "Our first artistic collaboration. A day-by-day record of changing shapes and colours. I'll need to get another tripod and maybe screw it to the floor."

"What will you be photographing?"

"Can't you guess? Anyway, you're going to be doing most of the work."

In fact Catherine is out of hospital the next day and he takes her home. He is able to drop everything else and spend some time with her. She has a rented room by the sea in a characterful but tacky village up the coast a little way. The houses stretch along either side of a straight road with shingle and sand down to the sea on one side and an expanse of low-lying marshland on the other. She is always moving to new addresses up and down the coast but she has stayed here longer than anywhere else.

She is a different person for him now, she needs looking-after. She really is in considerable discomfort and has difficulty moving so he cooks and tidies for her, goes away to walk on the beach when she wants quiet, and is there when she needs him. It is simple, there are no questions to be asked about this relationship for a while. He loves her. She needs him.

Her room is a bedsit occupying the attic-space of the house. It has no proper windows but instead a skylight high in the sloping ceiling which you can look out of only by standing on the table. As it is summer the window is open all the time. In the day they hear the sound of children playing on the beach but at night they hear the sea, especially when high tide brings the water up to the shingle ridge. They sleep under the window so that they can look up at the stars, lying on their backs without touching each other. She has nightmares of the accident and afterwards he comforts her with idle chatter until she can risk going back to sleep.

It should be a difficult time for them. She can't easily walk down the steep stairs so for days she doesn't leave the attic. She has only his company and can't see anything outside except the sky. It is also very hot in the attic. She is naked all the time as the movement of putting on or taking off clothes creates unnecessary pain. She stands in the shower from time to time to cool off. He goes out and swims in the sea until his body is chilled. Curiously they are very good together here. Their enforced proximity makes them take care to be both tolerant and thoughtful. It curbs their selfishness. This is a period of their relationship that stands apart from all their other times together.

Every day he takes photographs of her naked. Passionless studies of bruises. He is disturbed by this. She has lost weight and is now bony rather than slim and her bruises cover an increasingly large area of her body as they spread and change colour. He is fulfilled by looking after her but dislikes the ritual of setting up camera and lighting and then photographing someone who looks like a victim.

"You have no expression when I take the pictures," he says. "It's not you; it's some fragile poor thing who looks abused. It makes me feel guilty, like I'm taking advantage of you, or it's me who's done this to you."

"You're right. It's not me. When you get behind the camera I'm playing a part like someone in a movie. Or I'm a fictional character in a novel. Or actually just a still life. So don't worry. Anyway you should be honoured to be a part of my art – well I'm joking about that but not entirely joking. You're the only person who's ever been allowed into this part of my life."

She leaves the spot where she has stood each day to be photographed and walks towards him, "See? I'm me now."

Actually she is still moving quite carefully and awkwardly. She smiles and kisses him. He runs the tips of his fingers very gently across her shoulders and down her back. His touch is more chaste than sensual.

"You are very cool with me," she says, moving away, "do you find me ugly now?"

"No, I still think you're beautiful. And I like this time we're spending together. I love looking after you. It feels like the accident has actually given us something. I can't explain but it feels good."

She looks at him with concern. "Thank you for staying. The nightmares are terrible. It's as if images I won't allow into my consciousness in the day get through to me in the night. And you're wonderful being here for me when I wake. But I will need to be alone more in time, you understand that don't you?"

"Yes, I understand," he says sadly. "Well if you want to know the truth, I would like us to be able to live together some day. Everything we go through makes us closer. Makes us know each other more thoroughly. Makes our love more caring and not only a passion. This time is very special for me." He smiles, "Do you know we've spent five days and nights together without a row? It's got to be a record."

She moves her body lightly against his.

"Thank you for being so good. And you're right to be very gentle with me – it still hurts a lot. Laughing is the worst, or coughing. Do you notice how little I'm smoking these days?"

She stops speaking and is kissing the top of his shoulder and the side of his neck above his T-shirt.

"Crouch down a little," she says, "so that I can kiss you without stretching up and hurting myself."

He does as she asks and she kisses him, moving her lips across his, turning her head from side to side without moving her injured body. She runs her fingers down over his chest and stomach and then lower. They are both beginning to breathe a little faster and more deeply.

"I do want this," she says, moving her hand against him. "Will you sit on a chair for me and keep very still?"

He takes off his clothes and sits on a straight-backed chair in the middle of the room. She touches him a little and then eases herself down onto him carefully until he is inside her. She sighs and smiles at him. They are still for a while and then she allows herself a very little movement. She gives a small gasp of pain and then they sit for some time absolutely motionless, just absorbed in the pleasure of their bodies touching.

"Still life," she says.

The wind has picked up during the day and he must reef in the mainsail – if he keeps putting it off it will only become more difficult. He sets the self-steering mechanism and moves forward. Without him at the wheel the boat behaves badly, rolling and taking water onto the deck for the first time. He has chosen to wear a life-jacket today. Now, as the boat pitches suddenly and he is soaked by an awkwardly-met wave, he wonders if he should be wearing a harness and line. But he manages to bring the sail down and return safely. He has a better control of the boat now, she's keeling-over less and his job at the wheel is not so arduous. He realises that a further increase in the wind and waves will make it difficult to alter the sails at all so he uses a harness and short line, goes forward and takes in the jib. This is safer but the boat isn't set up to make the most speed, and back at the wheel he finds himself willing the wind to pick up a little more. His difficulties in these stronger winds and bigger waves are giving him a rush of adrenaline. There's an edge of fear, of excitement, and an awareness of his own skill.

When he decides to run back towards the shore he finds that he is fixing his course on a large radio mast that stands on a hill on this part of the coast. For half an hour, until he changes course again, his eyes are continually moving up from the waves to this landmark. He has for some time been so used to blocking out the feelings associated with this particular part of the landscape that it takes him a while to realise that uncomfortable memories and emotions are taking hold of him. Then he starts to intellectualise, to block out feelings with abstract thought. Landscape and memory have always had a hold on him. He knows that particular places, or even distant views of such places, will open up memories. After their relationship ended he would avoid certain places that stirred unwanted emotions. Sometimes he would get caught out by an unexpected view. But gradually new events left their imprint on the land. The old memories were steadily covered by new, the landscape defused. So why had a journey by boat along this coastline reactivated all this old stuff? Away from the land he should be emotionless, serene, safe. But these new views of the land from the sea have triggered memories, unearthed feelings. As he gradually comes to understand this it gets harder not to think of the winding road below the radio mast. Of that road in the dark, in the rain.

Sean and Catherine are in the pub with an assorted mixture of friends, some of them from the mediaeval music group. He is drinking steadily. They haven't discussed this but she is going through one of her no-alcohol phases and now as he sees her across the room drinking orange juice he assumes he can have a few drinks and she will drive. She has taken to spending part of the evening with the computer guys who sit in the corner. As her use of computer graphics in her art-work grows she increasingly needs to ask these guys for help. Asking for help seems to involve a degree of mild flirtation.

Drink is making him voluble and outgoing. He knows he is speaking loudly and that he has told a joke badly and made it seem more coarse than he intended. Fortunately he's able to see in the faces of his friends some clues about who he is tonight. He is someone who does not evoke warmth in other people at the moment. Their laughter at his jokes is polite and half-hearted so he decides to be quiet. As others speak he withdraws, the sound of his own voice echoing inside his head. A voice with a bitter edge to it, unpleasant. So he realises that things aren't going so well for him. For them. The sound of the jukebox, the conversation of his friends, their laughter, all this fades to no more than a backdrop for his thoughts. He thinks about their relationship, how they are different now, with this way of separating in the pub, talking to different people. She's across the room with others, other men, and she's animated, excited and beautiful. A seventies pop song is on the jukebox, like a voice in a dream telling him something he needs to know. Like a cheap jibe it makes him smile a little. 'Love hurts'. Exactly.

A year ago things were different. Then they were always together, some part of them touching, maybe holding hands. He remembers after dancing to some second-rate local band, she had sat on his lap, drunkenly loving. He ran his hands up and down her slim back and saw their friends smiling at them, reflecting back to him her happiness there. It was almost embarrassing for their friends sometimes, their public display of emotion. But people in general seemed to be with them, on their side. He doesn't feel they are on his side tonight. He wonders if she talks about him behind his back. For the first time he feels nostalgia for how they were. He drinks more beer and his mood changes to a pleasant melancholy. He even smiles a little, thinking of how they would kiss in public here in the pub. In his drunken reverie he's smiling into space, and across the room she catches his eye and smiles back. Time is being called and together they lurch into the street and make for her car. He's drunk enough to be unsteady and he gives her the keys.

"I hadn't really thought of driving," she says.

"But it's understood. I'm pissed. You've been on orange juice. It has to be you tonight."

As they drive through the small town he relaxes back into his seat and looks across at her profile lit by the street-lamps. He reflects on how much of all this is in his head. A drunken stillness of thought, a certain lucidity, allows him to understand that his feelings about her are poised. Tonight love might prevail. Or other feelings – disappointment, the beginnings of anger. But now he begins to feel good. They are out of the town and on a fast country road. There's a weird white light flashing into the car and it takes him a while to understand that it's the low moon, its light interrupted by passing roadside trees. Then the first drops of rain are falling on the windscreen. She turns on the wipers as the rain increases. He hears it loud on the roof of the car, together with the hiss of tyres on wet tarmac and the sound of water spraying up under the wheel arches. The moon has gone and he sees only the rain on the windscreen and the red light on the radio mast in front of them on the hill. He is soothed by it all. He is safe with the woman he loves, in a warm metal cocoon speeding through the wet night. He closes his eyes and enters a world of disembodied thoughts between sleep and waking. He loves the sensations of their movement, the way his body is pushed to the side as she takes the bends going up the hill. He can smell her there in the driver's seat beside him. Later they will lie in her bed, back to back, bottoms touching, drifting into sleep. He is nearly asleep now and is aware of the pleasant sensation of the car turning smoothly in an arc as if spinning rather than travelling forward.

But now they have stopped and the absence of motion wakes him abruptly. The car is still and silent. The engine has stopped and there's only the sound of rain falling heavily on the car and the road outside. There's enough light coming in for him to see her sitting still beside him, gripping the steering wheel tightly and staring straight ahead, transfixed. They are stationary on the wrong side of the road. He has a vague notion that they are facing back the way they have come, pointing at the bend they have just negotiated. The headlights of a large vehicle are coming towards them around the bend. Then a lorry appears, its wheels locking. It skids onto the other side of the road to pass them. He is suddenly clear-headed. When the lorry has passed he will ask her to get the car moving again, and away from the bend. But the lorry has skidded back onto their side of the road, its headlights shining very brightly on them for a moment. The impact takes his breath away.

EIGHT

Julian and I have stayed on the land later than usual and he has been kind enough to give me some supper before I go. Now we've finished eating and sit outside for a moment. The sun has gone down behind the hill but it will remain light for most of the next hour. It is still warm outside, a fine evening; being here at this time of day is a novelty. Today we've pulled and hoed a great many weeds, the crops look better for our work, and the tiredness of physical exertion is a good sensation.

"Some of the sailing stuff is crap," Julian says, pleasantly.

"What?"

"In your novel. The stuff about sailing isn't very good. You'll have to change it, you know."

"I don't think it really matters. The boat is only a vehicle."

"Not a very good vehicle if you were trying to sail it like..." Julian doesn't complete his sentence. He smiles and I begin to laugh.

"Okay," he says, "you mean a vehicle for telling the story. So perhaps I am a bit too – what is it you call me? – literal-minded, sometimes. But you haven't done much sailing, have you?"

"I went out once and I didn't like it. It took all day to get nowhere. But I've got a good book about it out of the library."

The phone rings and Julian goes in to answer it. When he comes out he tells me that we're needed.

"Tom Owen has lost a valuable animal in the woods. I'm going to help them look for it. Will you come too? It's part of being in a farming community. We all rally round at a time like this."

The animal in question is a dairy cow that has broken out of its field. If several of us spread out and search we will find it before dark. So Julian and I drive over to this place and meet up with a team of neighbours who have arrived to help. Gareth and Olivia are there with one of their sons who is home from college. We all walk down to the field that the cow escaped from and the farmer makes a plan for us to divide up and search. The woods spread across the damp floor of the valley, looking dark and forbidding in the fading light. Everybody is cheerfully helpful but I feel tired and resent being here. I need a long hot bath. We divide up and walk into the woods. I didn't listen too carefully to the instructions but I understand that if one of us finds the animal that person calls out and we all go and help to chase the cow out of the woods. Then we can go home.

I walk steadily into the trees, trying to keep the people either side of me in sight. Farmers generally wear drab clothing. I always thought it signified a lack of *joie de vivre* – now I understand it's camouflage to make them difficult to see in the woods at dusk. From time to time I do get a glimpse of the man on my right. I am irritable, waiting for someone to find the animal and call out for us to return. There are two characteristics of these woods: either the trees are close together and it's difficult to see in the faint light; or they're more spread out and it's lighter but there are more brambles. Actually there are other characteristics. Increasingly as I get further down into the valley, there are areas that are wet underfoot and very unpleasant to walk through. And there are rocky outcrops that you wouldn't expect here. I navigate around two of these outcrops and cross a stream. Then there's another stream; the two must join up close by. More brambles. More rocks. Wet underfoot. Another small stream. Okay, it's getting dark, I haven't seen or heard anything of the others for a while, I'm in danger of getting lost and need to turn back. I soon arrive at the confluence of the two streams so I know where I am. And then, after a little time has passed, I have to admit that I don't know where I am. I feel angry with myself for not taking care, also frustrated and something else I don't want to admit. A little bit frightened. It isn't completely dark and although I can't see the ground very well I can make out the shapes of trees.

It is a very still evening, no movement of wind in the leaves above me, almost no sound. This is one of those fecund verdant places where mosses cover the ground and spread up onto the trunks and branches of trees. Where the brambles are absent there are bushy ferns. All this vegetation absorbs sound and light. Perhaps it's a long way from being dark outside but it's gloomy here. I have to concentrate on deciphering the shapes and patterns of things around me. There is just a tiny glimmer of light reflected off the small stream in front of me.

I hear a movement behind and I turn to see part of the mossy rock outcrop detach itself and move towards me. Its feet make sucking noises in the mud. When it gets closer it stretches its head forward and makes a lowing sound.

"Hello, old girl," I say, the sort of words I imagine farmers saying to their favourite cows. The animal's ears come forward to my voice then take turns to fold back and check for noise from behind. I watch as the cow continues this elaborate semaphore of movements, first one ear forward and one back, then all change, now both forward, now both back as I approach and it becomes frightened of me. I can smell the sweet odour of the animal's hide, a good smell, not the one usually associated with livestock.

"Doctor Livingstone, I presume," I say and the cow backs off, shaking its head as if bothered by flies. I realise that I've achieved the thing that we came into the woods to do. I shout to attract the attention of the others. This sound disturbs the cow and she scampers away. It seems that my call won't carry far through all this verdure and anyway it frightens the cow off. I have to carry on trying to find my way out of the wood. I'm happier now, the meeting has cheered me up. This has a Midsummer Night's Dream feel to it. A little magical and absurd. I'm having a night out.

As I walk up the hill between the trees – back, I hope, the way I came – the cow follows me, lowing occasionally. So I have a big furry friend in the woods. This is the nearest I've come to making friends with an animal. This big thing (there's something nice about it being so big) is choosing my company. I'm decisive in my direction now and so it's not long before I get to the edge of the woods, a fence with a road on the other side. I climb over and sit at the edge of the road, wondering where I am in relation to Gareth's or Julian's farm. My big friend watches me from the other side of the fence. I start walking along, pausing from time to time to allow Livingstone, as she's now called, to catch up. Then there are headlights and a Land Rover pulls up beside me. The two men in the front seats are grinning.

"We made a bet," Julian says, "as to where you would turn up. I decided that you would be at the furthest point from where we started. Gareth owes me a fiver."

I'm embarrassed. "Thanks for coming to find me," I say.

"I know how disorienting those woods can be," Gareth says. "Very easy to get lost in. You're not the first. But we haven't found the cow, I'm sorry to say."

"Oh really. What, nobody's seen her at all?"

"No," he says, but he can see that I'm smiling.

"Gentlemen, can I introduce my friend Livingstone?" I say, and direct their attention to the cow standing motionless in the half-dark behind the fence.

"Well I never," Gareth says.

Julian goes up the lane a little way and cuts a piece out of the fence with some pliers. Gareth and I follow on slowly, Livingstone keeping up with us, and with some cajoling we get her out of the woods and onto the road. Julian drives off to tell Tom Owen, leaving Gareth and me to get her into a well-fenced field. I lead the way as she seems to follow me. Gareth walks behind her, moving her on with a hard slap on her flanks when she stops to graze on the roadside grasses. It takes some time to get her into an appropriate field. Then Gareth and I walk back through the fields above the woods, under the stars, on dry ground, free of brambles and tree branches.

"You realise you're an honorary local now?" Gareth says. "Of course only time will tell if you'll be remembered as 'that strange man who got lost in the woods' or as 'the man who found Tom

Owen's best cow'. She's worth a few bob, you know. You've done a good evening's work."

"I've enjoyed myself actually," I say. "It's been a little adventure. But I like being here in the open again and not in those woods. I can see why they were frightening places in times past."

There is no moon tonight and in the clear air the stars are shining with hints of colour. "That star there is very red," I say to Gareth, hardly expecting him to be interested.

"It's Mars, the red planet," he says. "It's always down on the horizon at this time of night."

We walk on in silence. I think that Gareth, like me, is enjoying this summer evening under the stars. We climb a fence into the next field. A big white owl comes out of the wood below and flies up past us as if to take a look. You can hear the silence of its movement through the air.

"Barn owl," Gareth says, then after a pause, "What do you do with yourself John, when you're not working for Julian?"

My preoccupations must seem petty to him, someone who works hard to make a living on the land.

"I take photographs and I do some painting. And I write. Play music. I used to be involved with a theatre company."

As if to add some sort of status to this I add, "I went to art college many years ago." I feel he must disapprove of this self-indulgent lifestyle.

"Have you always farmed here?" I say, assuming that it's the only life he's known.

"No, not at all. But some of my neighbours have. I've been here twenty years but I'm still a newcomer to them."

"What did you do before?"

"You won't believe me," he says.

Gareth has a soft deep voice in the dark. He's a physically powerful man, though very gentle mannered. He has a face that looks lived-in and he doesn't always look entirely happy. But now in the dark I have only his voice to go by and there's something youthful and enthusiastic about him. Also a warmth. I feel that I might have my preconceptions of him turned around.

"Go on."

"Well, I was many years in New Zealand after agri college. Did a lot of shearing and also some drinking. Then I was in a band out there – lead singer. Toured Australia twice supporting big US bands who came over."

"Wow. Well I do believe you but I couldn't have guessed. What happened? Did you ever make an album?"

"It was very exciting, and big stuff for your ego. A little bit of fame. Lots of drugs of course. We started making an album but we self-destructed. Then I inherited some money and drank quite a bit of it. I had to sort myself out. Farming is sanity for me. And Olivia of course."

"Did you write the songs?" I ask. I want to know if Gareth has a creative side, in which case I suppose we have something in common. And maybe he doesn't think of me as a waster.

"A few," he says. "You know, I think of those days very rarely now. It must seem boring to you, me being a farmer. I love the work though. It's fulfilling. Can you imagine that?"

I can't imagine wanting to spend so much time doing the dirty chores of farm work and nothing else. I enjoy being a part-time employee, a dilettante worker on the land.

"Maybe," I say. And I'm so amazed that Gareth has had this other life that I can't think of what else to say. The rest of the way back we are silent, enjoying the night. In the lane by his farm we separate; I have to go back to Julian's and get my car.

"Thank you for helping our farming-folk out," Gareth says, a good humoured irony in his voice. "Remember you're one of us now."

There is just a steady north-westerly, and the sea is relatively calm. He has pushed slowly out into the bay, making some distance as the hours pass. Now he turns and sets the mainsail to one side of the mast, the jib to the other, and goose-wings towards and along the coast in the direction of home. The sky is clear but he doesn't have the benefit of the sun's direct heat as he stands in the shadow of the mainsail. The sea glistens with sunlight ahead of him. To each side it is a deep dark blue.

A smooth movement in the water on the port beam attracts his attention. He glances to his left from time to time hoping to see more. Then he sees a dark curved back and dorsal fin as a dolphin breaches. Then two more arch out of the water on the starboard bow. It is still for a moment then the sea comes alive all around him. It is one of those days when a large group of dolphins – just for fun, it seems – has come to play around the boat. The wind is picking up and he is moving faster. The dolphins keep pace with him effortlessly, appearing and disappearing constantly on each side of the boat. Sometimes one will leave the water completely and return with a splash, otherwise there's just a constant movement of arching backs and dorsal fins. Now on the starboard beam there are two travelling close together, a mother and her small metre-long calf, visible sometimes just below the surface of the water, now breaching together before diving out of sight. He sets the self-steering mechanism and can now watch them more thoroughly. To be in such company lifts his spirits enormously. They seem happy, playful and exuberant. Two dolphins have moved into the bow-wave, one either side of the bow; he can just see them from his position at the wheel. With the self-steerer on he can go forward and get closer. He lies stretched out on his stomach right in the bow of the boat, his face half-jutting out over the edge, salt-spray constantly wetting him. Right below and very close, two, and now three, dolphins speed through the water. He could almost reach down and touch them as they rise up. He has never been so close to them before. He is elated, these big wild joyful creatures have chosen to keep him company. Now they change places with each other, speedily criss-crossing under the bow. It seems that they have come to entertain him, to show off, to cheer him up. Then he sees their dark shapes speeding away to starboard, first two from the bow wave, then the other one, and then they have all gone and he is alone.

He goes back to the wheel and gets the boat back on course again. He adjusts the sails. Then he looks carefully at the sea all around hoping to see his friends again. For some time he anticipates their presence but he knows that they will soon be far away. He doesn't see them again but they have made his day. It was a privilege to be in their company.

Sean walks along the prom and looks down at the sandy beach and the small waves gently breaking. It is his habit to be on time and he looks at his watch. There is always a heightened sense of anticipation when he walks here. The excitement of being about to see her again. The people that he passes here seem happier than those in other parts of the small town. There's a family in front of him, a couple and two young boys who are running across the prom and leaping out onto the sand. They have a tiny puppy that chases around excitedly but is too scared of the height to jump off onto the sand with the boys. Now the man is running and jumping too. The woman looks on indulgently, smiling.

The sun comes out from behind a cloud and is reflected off the windows of the large Victorian houses across the road. Her car, the VW Beetle, is parked in its usual place. He crosses the road, walks up to her door and rings the bell. Sometimes she won't be there even though they've agreed a time. He has tried to explain that he finds this upsetting, his anticipation disappointed. What irritates him is her dismissal of this – it's his problem and it's not something she will consider; if he continues to bring it up he's making trouble. So he is a little irritated as he waits. If she is there she will open the sash window and throw down the keys so that he can let himself in. But this time there is no answer. At this point in their relationship their happiness is so great that disappointments are keenly felt. They are both over-sensitive. He wishes she would be more considerate.

He walks away along the prom and past the pier to the castle. The sea glistens in the sun, flickering pinpoints of light coming off the small waves. He looks at his watch often and thinks of how unaware of time he is when they are together. He finds himself thinking of a guitar he once bought. It was very expensive and the best musical instrument he had ever owned. He could play simple phrases over and over again just to enjoy the ringing tone and the harmonics sounding at the back of each note. One string buzzed against the frets a little in some positions – it made him quite angry. He understands why he's thinking of this. Ordinariness is easy, undemanding and comfortable. But when something in your life is extraordinary the flaws are keenly felt and hurtful. She is never on time, he is too much upset, and that's how it is. He mustn't make an issue of it.

He sits on the castle wall above the beach trying not to be irritable and trying not to look at his watch. He stares at the sea, noticing the changing colour as he turns his head gradually away from the bright sun, seeing for a moment some wrongly shaped waves. These waves come and go quickly. They have dorsal fins. He is now scrutinising the water intently and hoping to see more or to see them closer. Then he runs down the path to the edge of the beach. There must be six – no, ten – or maybe a dozen – dolphins swimming backwards and forwards a little way out from the beach, their arched backs smoothly breaking out of the water at unpredictable intervals. One leaps from the water and re-enters with a splash. It makes him hold his breath. Then another has leapt and turned in the air. Now they are quieter, just big curved shiny backs and dorsal fins emerging now and then, sometimes close enough to the shore to give him a real impression of their size. He realises that there are people walking past him who haven't noticed them. He feels that he should tell everyone to look but he thinks his excitement will make him seem a little mad. He has rarely seen these big playful animals from the shore. He feels privileged and happy.

He stares out to sea as the dolphins move away. Two hands are placed either side of his waist and he feels the warmth of breath, then the touch of lips, on the back of his neck. He turns on the spot and they exchange hugs and kisses. Catherine wants to talk and wants to kiss him too and so her words are spoken with her lips close to his, odd words and phrases breathed to him intermittently, punctuated at random with kisses, the tip of her tongue on his.

"I wanted you to see them too, I wanted to run back to the house and get you. But what if you weren't there? They are beautiful animals, aren't they?"

They don't want to let go of each other and so turn together, their bodies still touching, like awkward dancers. They alternate between glancing at the sea and long speechless looks at each other. They rock from side to side and kiss, bumping into an old man and smiling apologies. They rub themselves against each other playfully. Then they turn and walk briskly and decidedly, hand in hand, smiling, back to her one room flat above the prom.

"You write your name on all your album covers. That's good – it means people who borrow them might give them back one day. But there are lots with Jennifer Thomas written on them. Did she give you all these?"

Sean is going through Catherine's record collection and she watches and smiles. He is naked except for a T-shirt worn back-to-front, she is naked and curled up sitting on a chair wrapped in a duvet.

"Your willy stays nice and plump after we've made love," she says.

"Are these really all your records? I'm very impressed by your eclecticness – is that a word?"

"Don't change the subject. I want to talk about your body."

"Okay, you talk. I'll look at the records."

"It must be fun having a part of your body that changes all the time."

"I see you've got the White Album but not Abbey Road. That's strange. And I thought we were going to be soul mates."

She is laughing to herself. She gets up and sits on the floor close to him, staring concentratedly at his cock.

"What are you doing?" he asks.

"It's an experiment," she says, "to see if I can make it bigger just by staring."

He tries to read the sleeve notes of an old soul album. There's a song called 'You've Got it Bad Girl'. That seems about right. She's still staring and he tries to think of something to distract himself, to fully occupy his mind. 'I wonder who did Stevie Wonder's hair like that' he thinks. 'Why does he dress all in brown?' He is aware that it's no use. She's laughing happily.

"It's working," she says. "The power of thought."

She touches her lips to the end of his swelling penis and then goes back to her chair to huddle again under the duvet. He smiles to himself and shrugs his shoulders.

"Jennifer Thomas again," he says. "Who is Jennifer Thomas."

Catherine sits quietly for a while, lost in thought, smiling and then frowning. She gets up from the chair, puts the duvet on the bed and gets dressed. He stops looking at her records and CDs and follows her example, getting dressed properly with his T-shirt on the right way round. She opens the sash window a bit wider. The breeze coming in off the sea lifts the curtains.

"The dolphins have a beneficial effect on us, I think. And Jennifer Thomas was me."

"You, how come?"

"When I left my marriage I changed both names. I didn't want to go back to my maiden name and I wanted to change my first name too. I wanted to be entirely and only me."

"Are we talking about this stuff now?" he says.

"Maybe."

"I admire you, you know. The self-made woman," he says. "I understand why you won't do it but I love you enough to want us to be married. And I dream of having children one day."

"I'm sorry," she says. It's one of the few times he's ever heard her say that word.

"Marriage is abhorrent to me," she says. "I don't understand why you want it. Why?"

"So that we're always together. If something is so good, you want it to go on, don't you? Is the idea of being faithful to me abhorrent as well?"

"No, it isn't. I do love you. I will be faithful to you."

They are both a little agitated now. He looks wistful, sad. She lights a cigarette.

"Can we leave this subject?" she says.

He goes to the window and leans out. Then he turns to her, "You know a lot of people didn't see the dolphins," he says. "They were just walking past. Being there with you was very special."

"Last week I was on my own there, by the castle," she says. "The sea was very flat and shiny, metallic looking – like mercury or something. Very different from today. As I sat there two swans came around the point, sitting on the water and paddling with their feet. Why they didn't get off the water and fly I don't know. They were white, of course. And feathery. And *on* the water not *in* it. They swam past me and I watched. They went across the same piece of water that the dolphins were in today. Thinking of it now it's hard to imagine how they could be in that same place. I mean, it's hard to believe they're even from the same planet. So weird that they inhabit the same medium."

He looks out of the window again but the sea doesn't look particularly special to him now. The sun is high behind thin cloud and everything he can see has a colourless uniform quality. There is a contrast between what he sees and the tone of the words she has just spoken. Below the window there is a narrow strip of busy holiday activity, traffic in slow procession along the road, large numbers of people walking along the prom eating ice-creams or chips. Then the small stretch of beach that isn't covered by the tide. And the sea, very still and characterless, like a badly painted backdrop to a second-rate play. Right now he longs for a wilder place and a different time of year. And for less of the bustle of common-place humanity.

He picks up a photograph that lies on the desk by the window. It's a picture of someone he hasn't seen before, a man with cropped hair and a square jaw, looking at the camera without expression.

"Who's this?" he asks.

"My brother, Tim," she says, smiling.

"He looks like a tough cookie to me."

"Well he isn't. You'll see."

"I'll see?"

"Yes, he's coming to stay soon. That's why I got his picture out."

"How long is he staying for?" he asks.

"I can't say. My brother isn't someone you can pin down."

"Days or weeks?"

"I really don't know," she says happily. "But you'd better get on with him."

He looks uncertain.

"Really, it's important. He's a very special person in my life. I looked after him a lot when my mother was ill. We've been very close."

"Is he much younger than you then?"

"Ten years."

"It will be interesting to meet him," he says without enthusiasm.

"I think you two will get on. Everybody likes my brother. They like him too much sometimes."

She smiles excitedly. But he feels uncomfortable and makes no attempt to hide it from her. She doesn't notice; he is already a little bit invisible to her.

"I think I like having you all to myself," he says.

She looks at him critically for a moment.

"Yes," she says, "I know you do."

NINE

She has left the town and moved to the village that stretches along a shingle ridge between the sea and the marshes. She is excited about the amount of space that she now has for her work and is not bothered by the fact that her attic flat has no proper window but only skylights. She likes the pub which is almost opposite and which sometimes serves after hours. Most of all she is happy that her brother is coming to visit her for the first time in years.

Sean and Catherine are at the small village station waiting for his train. The single platform faces away from the village and the sea and so they find themselves looking inland, across the tracks to the marshes and the bleak hills beyond. They are the only people there.

"Busy today," he says.

She looks at him inquiringly.

"Three crows," he says. "Oh, and two sheep in the field over there. I don't know what your brother is going to make of this place. Straight from London to the edge of the known world. A bit of a culture shock."

He stops pacing and sits down next to her on the bench. He is upright and uncomfortable, like someone waiting for an interview. Beside him she is slumped and at ease, her legs stretched out in front of her. She has chosen her clothes carefully and creatively today. Instead of her usual scruffy jeans she wears a short skirt over leggings. Her hair is tied into two high bunches with odd coloured pieces of cloth.

On time for once, the single carriage train slows and stops in front of them. A window opens and a young man looks out. Then he opens the door, tumbles onto the platform with his bags, and smiles. He pushes the carriage door shut behind him with his foot and runs forward to hug Catherine and shake hands with Sean.

"It didn't think this was the place," Tim says. "There's nothing here at all." The train pulls away and he looks at the empty landscape with real surprise. "I wasn't going to get off. You didn't tell me you lived in the wilderness."

She shows him to the door that leads out of the station and towards the village.

"Thank God," he says. "There are buildings. And there's the sea."

Sean looks at the younger man carefully. He is quite different from how he had imagined him. He is about the same height as his sister and has some of her expressions and movements. He wears neatly-pressed jeans and a white T-shirt and his perfect physique looks like something he got from the gym rather than the workplace. His hair is cropped as it is in the photo Sean has seen, but with a little tuft sticking up at the front. There is something macho about the way he is dressed but feminine about the way he moves. And he wears a necklace of large coloured wooden beads that should look incongruous but doesn't.

They help him with his bags and walk first to the beach. The tide is very far out and the sand stretches far and wide in front of them.

"Yes," Tim says. "Okay."

His eyes are unable to quite take in the scale and the sheer absence of anything in front of him. It is as if he is used to seeing only the things that enclose him, nothing of space or distance. They walk through the village to her flat. Inside and surrounded by her things, he seems more at home. He looks at her paintings and picks up her bass guitar. She makes tea for everyone.

"I never heard you in that band," he says. "Did you manage to record anything before the split?"

"No," she says. "And I never play now because I need to be single-minded. I need to concentrate on my painting."

He switches on the amp and sits on top of it with his legs crossed, tuning-up and playing riffs and snatches of melody. He talks and plays at the same time, only stopping to drink the tea she has given him. He talks about life in the city, part-time jobs that didn't last, creative projects that fell flat, dingy apartments that he had to leave, all of it told with good-natured smiles and jokes.

"Wait," he says. "Listen I think I've got something."

He concentrates and plays a continuous flowing line of strange melody in a minor key, only occasionally having to search for a note, mostly finding the tune without effort.

"Do you know what this is?" he asks. "It's from the Bach solo cello stuff, I think it's the one in D minor. Am I playing in D minor?"

She looks at him with admiration. "This is my brother," she says to Sean. "Talented, spoilt and beautiful – just as he always was."

"I didn't know you played bass too," Sean says.

"I don't really. But I can get a tune out of most things."

"Tim studied viola at the Royal College before he became a committed layabout," she says. "Did you manage a whole year?" she asks him.

"Nearly."

"Never mind. Tell me about that job in the music shop. What happened there?"

"Oh, I liked it. I could show off. Playing all sorts of instruments, messing around with fancy keyboards, guitars. I sold things okay. Sometimes people spent a lot more money than they planned to. So I was useful and they let me get away with being less than perfect at time-keeping and so on."

"You always did manage to charm your way along," she says.

"Ah, well I took it too far. I borrowed a keyboard for a gig without asking and got caught smuggling it back in the next morning. It didn't look at all damaged to me."

"So that was it?"

"Yes, but I had a rich girlfriend by then and it didn't seem important. She took me to New York, I sent you a card didn't I?"

"You did. And you said you were a gigolo."

"Well she was quite a bit older than me. But we were soul mates too."

"Was she a musician?"

"No, we were soul mates in a cocaine-snorting sort of way. It was too wild."

"Too wild for *you?*" she says, incredulous.

He looks across at Sean for a moment.

"I'll tell you about it Cath," he says, "but not now. You tell me all of your stuff. How come you're always moving to a new address?"

Sean feels he is superfluous for the time being. They are too excited about seeing each other to include him in the conversation.

"I'm going for a walk on the beach," he says, and leaves quietly.

Outside the fresh air feels particularly good. Two people smoking in that room is one more than he is used to. But the beach and the sea won't hold his interest. The day has gone rather grey. The tiniest most unenthusiastic of waves break listlessly onto the sand. He thinks they look like a bunch of old dishcloths being shaken out. Sean hasn't really warmed to her brother, and he's upset that this man's presence will disrupt his relationships with Catherine. He walks along the sea's edge kicking a deflated plastic football that has been washed ashore. The few words the brother has said do make him seem like a spoilt and selfish man. But wait a minute – isn't he being a bit like that himself now? He decides to do something positive rather than simply sulk on the beach. He checks his wallet and walks off the beach between the houses and towards the village shop. He buys some food for the three of them to eat together that evening and takes it back to the flat.

He must knock a few times before she answers. He tries to smile away the little feeling of irritation that is creeping over him; he knows that he is pleased to see her looking so happy. When he enters the room behind her, the brother is on the edge of the bed with an old acoustic guitar of hers. She returns to her bass and they carry on where they left off, trying to remember songs from their childhood, the songs that the brother knows from his older sister's record collection.

"Shall I make supper for us all?" Sean says.

She smiles and nods and carries on singing. He peels potatoes and puts them on to cook, prepares a salad, checks that the eggs in the fridge haven't gone bad. Their music sounds good. He would like her to play music with him again – it has been a long time since that part of their relationship faded out. The three of them eat together and he tries his best. He asks her brother questions and tries to find something in common with him. When the meal is finished, Tim unzips his backpack and carefully takes everything out. There are neatly pressed and folded clothes which he lays out on the sofa beside him. Then a collection of necklaces and bracelets made from wood and unlikely scrap materials. He takes off the necklace that he is wearing and with unselfconscious care replaces it with one made from what appear to be parts of a bicycle gear changer.

"Two presents," he says and calls his sister over. First he gives her a sealed plastic bag containing a large lump of hash. Then he passes her a cardboard tube that she finds contains a number of sheets of manuscript paper.

"A bit like a string quartet but with words in the second movement. A woman's voice. I've dedicated it to you because you always encouraged me. I don't think that I'll ever get it played. Anyway it's yours."

She wraps her arms around him and kisses him on the cheek. She turns over the pages of his composition with a certain reverence. Then she opens the plastic bag and sniffs the hash.

"Shall we start on this now?" she asks him.

"That was my plan," he says.

He rolls a joint while she tidies and does the washing-up. She can't smoke with wet hands so he holds it to her lips. Sean watches this strange intimacy with disquiet. He refuses the brother's offer of some of the joint, takes a beer instead and sits watching her. She is standing at the sink with a look of domesticity that he has not seen before. She turns and looks at her brother stretched out on the sofa with his collection of jewellery. She smiles indulgently. She is a different person now. She has never been as easy-going and tolerant towards Sean as she is to her younger brother. The next time Tim offers him some of the joint he accepts. It is very strong and changes his perceptions straight away. He sees at the sink not the woman he would normally recognise as his lover but someone with a quite different manner. Like somebody's mum. Of course that's it. She had to look after her brother a lot when he was little. She was partly a mother to this spoilt young man sitting on the sofa opposite him. He understands. He values seeing this new part of her character. But he has other thoughts. That indulgence and kindness isn't a part of her relationship with him and he wishes it was.

"Is there a night-life around here?" Tim asks. "What do you do for sociable kicks?"

"We can try the pub," she says.

It is a Friday night, already the little pub opposite her flat is busy and they are lucky to get a table in the corner. From here Tim takes a very obvious delight in watching everyone else. There are locals, one group of which are perhaps farmers. There are academic looking types who are maybe from the local university. And there are the bohemian incomers, scruffy creative people, some in brightly-coloured clothing. Catherine tries to explain to her brother the sort of lifestyle that people have here. When Sean contributes to the picture he finds that he is describing the place as much as the people: the hills, the coastline, the sea's unpredictable character. Her brother is only half-listening, and interrupts to ask his sister about another group of people coming in through the door. Then they are talking about childhood holidays at the seaside and the things they remember about their parents' difficult marriage.

The curious thing for Sean is how much brother and sister resemble each other. They have shared mannerisms and ways of speaking. And as the evening moves on, he finds that he is looking more and more at the brother, fascinated by what he sees of her in him. And more than this; something about Tim holds Sean's attention. Sean has a vague memory of a play he once saw: one character had a charisma that drew you to him even when he was at the side of the stage and others were speaking. Then Sean remembers that it wasn't a play at all – it was one of the very few times that he had been to see a ballet. There was one dancer, a man, who had a languorous grace and beauty that made it difficult to look at anyone else on the stage. There's some of that in her brother. And he is young, perhaps the youngest person in the room. His face has an open expression and his pleasure in being surrounded by other people is obvious. When he goes to the bar he is drawn into conversation with the people beside him. He is showing someone the necklace that he wears, explaining how he made it. Later, a man who by his manner might be gay comes over with a drink, just one, puts it on the table in front of the brother and goes away without saying anything.

"It's just because he's beautiful," Catherine explains. "It happens all the time."

For two days Sean has kept away from the sea, and from her and her young brother. Now he arrives at the flat in the middle of the morning. She lets him in unenthusiastically.

"I want to work," she says. "I need to start again on this painting but he won't stop talking to me."

She looks towards her brother stretched indolently on the sofa, a cup of coffee in his hand. She smiles, exasperated rather than angry.

"Take him away please. Go on, you two, go and see some of the world out there and let me work."

The young man looks up at Sean. "Okay, let's go. Do what you want with me and we'll let Cath get on."

They wander out onto the beach, the younger man good-natured and relaxed, the older one uncertain, smiling to cover his discomfort, aware that this is not what he came here to do. The tide is out and they walk down to the sea's edge. The water is still and glossy in the hazy sunshine; patches of silver light move across the surface, a small swell breaks cleanly onto the sand. They walk along together but in rather different worlds. Sean wants to talk about the sea's different moods, about the outlines of distant hills that are as familiar to him as old friends, about the tides and the wind. The young man beside him looks at the very edge of the water and at the sand in front of his feet. It is frustrating to be here with someone who is oblivious to what should be so stimulating. It seems pointless to try to tell him what to look at, to show him the world that is right here in front of him. So they say little. They walk for a while.

"I'm okay with silence," the young man says. "It's good. She's right – I do talk too much. But this is nice. Thank you for bringing me out here."

In front of them now is a channel of water, flowing out to sea from a pool left by the retreating tide. They are diverted away from the edge of the sea and up the beach towards the dry sand. Here the young man discovers the strand-line, the strip of debris left when the tide turned and went out. He pushes at some seaweed with the toe of one shoe. Then he bends and sorts through the stuff with his hands. Now he has stopped to examine the shell of a sea urchin and soon becomes engrossed in the smaller details of coloured pebbles and shells. He kneels down. Sean sits on the dry sand close by and watches. Tim becomes a child. He starts with hesitant interest, then grows excited, and at last becomes totally absorbed. He starts to make collections of small pieces of smooth driftwood, stones with interesting markings, multi-coloured shells. When he looks at the other man it is with the smile of a child sharing his pleasure with an adult.

"It's like the flea-market," he says. "Better maybe. Look at these."

In the palm of his hand are some tiny limpet shells, each one marked with blue lines radiating out from the centre.

"There's a place near here where you can find cowry shells," Sean says.

"You're taking the piss."

"No, it's true. But not the big ones you get in the tropics, little ones the size of the things you've got in your hand. Do you want to see them?"

They still have little to say to each other but now they are companionable rather than awkward. They cut through the sand dunes, disturbing rabbits that are grazing there, and come to the mouth of a wide estuary. Again Sean is struck by the young man's inability to take in what is for him an impressive scene, a vast space of sand and water between the hills, illuminated by shafts of soft light that come down through gaps in the clouds. There are a number of wooden bollards here that have been dug into the sand to stop vehicles driving up into the dunes. Sean takes his friend to the hollows that are made when very high tides swirl around the posts. He starts to look for cowry shells among the detritus left here by the sea.

"They're always here," he says. "Nowhere else."

The young man bends and searches too. There are hundreds of tiny dull spire-shaped shells, small sticks and pieces of seaweed, and a few perfect small shiny cowry shells that he begins to collect. He is soon absorbed in the task. Sean, feeling that this will take some time, climbs to the top of one of the higher dunes to look at the view. The two men are in different worlds now. Sean is in a grand landscape of estuary and wild hills, Tim in a world of small beauty, as a child would be. When he has finished he climbs up to where Sean is sitting.

"You knew they were there," he says. "I'm impressed." He shows him the handful of shells he has collected. "I think I'll give them to Cath. And right now I'd like to take you to the pub and treat you to lunch."

They walk back along the beach to the village. Tim has found an old plastic bucket to carry his collection. Facing this way the sun is on their faces and Tim takes off his shirt. Sean notices a tattoo on his shoulder, a small bird, something like a swallow. There are things he wants to ask the young man.

"You know, Catherine won't talk about her childhood," he says. "Maybe that's okay, I shouldn't pry."

"I have lots of happy memories," Tim says, "but it was difficult for her. Mum was ill, mentally ill. Cath had to take a lot of responsibility. She looked after me when I was little. I think she was very determined, later on, to put it all behind her. To live for herself. Dad was a bit of a bastard. A womaniser. He was at the root of the problems, I think. I love him still but I never see him – does that make any sense? Cath won't have anything to do with him."

"And your mother?"

"Hasn't Cath told you? It was later on, after we'd all gone our separate ways. You really don't know this do you?"

"She's never spoken to me about your parents."

"Our mother took her own life."

They walk on in silence for a while.

"You'd better not tell her I told you. Not for the moment."

Silence again.

"Do you love my sister?" Tim says.

"Yes, we're very in love."

"She's more vulnerable than you think. I hope you're a good guy."

"I love her, but it's not easy."

A pattern develops as the days pass. She wants to work and the two men must potter about on the beach. Back at the flat, Tim makes necklaces with pieces of plastic bucket, huge dog-whelk shells, small driftwood sticks worn smooth by the sea. He wears a new one every evening in the pub, completely at home there, unconcerned about the effect of his eccentricity. People like him. They buy him drinks and they will help him home if he has had too much and can't walk properly.

The two men spend some time together on the beach or on the rocks below the cliffs. Each day, the sea has left something different for them. They spend hours looking in rock pools and making up names for the strange creatures they find. One day, after a storm, there are a large number of dead dog-fish along the strand-line, spotty little sharks beginning to decay and stink already. There are also lots of cockles that have been scoured up out the sand and washed in by the big waves. Their shells gape, and protruding from each one is a pink piece of flesh of unguessable purpose. It is like a finger or a foot or a sucker or something used for feeding. Or they are sexual parts of ambiguous gender, maybe male and female in the same organ. Tim is pleased to see the beach littered with, as he puts it, 'sex and death'. The beach does seem to hold more life when Tim is there. It has been a relatively barren place for Sean. Now, under the close investigation of the young man, it teems with organisms that can't be explained or understood. There are things that seem to be plants but are perhaps animals, things that might easily be either alive or dead, things without shape.

Catherine has little time for her lover now. If he is with her then Tim is there too. At night Tim sleeps on the sofa. If Sean stays, then he and Catherine share the bed chastely, unable to make love with someone else in the room. One night they have gone to bed very drunk and stoned and Sean has a dream that he is, in some way, part of the revolting fecundity of the seashore. He sees the gaping cockle-shells with their pink appendages; the tentacles of sea-anemones grasping their prey; jellyfish swimming in slow-motion; starfish, sea-slugs, seaweed all around him. He wakes to find that they have started to make love, she is on top, pushing herself down and against him. He is revolted and terribly aroused at the same time; he must carry on with what they have started in their sleep.

There is a note from her brother in the morning. He has gone into town to spend some money. He has borrowed a T-shirt of hers because he doesn't have a clean one of his own. Sean is slightly disgusted by the vague aftertaste of his strange dream. He showers, hoping to wash away his discomfort but not succeeding. He eats breakfast alone while she watches from the bed. She makes a mock sad face to cover her real sadness at his being so cool and distant today, when they could be in bed, cuddling up to each other or making love. He has read Tim's note aloud to her; now his mind dwells on her brother's presence, forgetting that he is his friend.

"He borrows your clothes – that's good," he says with a note of bitterness.

"What's the problem with that?" she asks.

"Well you never let me borrow them."

She laughs. "You're too big, silly. You'd destroy anything of mine you tried to get on."

He should be able to laugh with her but the word 'silly' sounds patronising, a put-down.

"Or anything," he says. "I guess that's what I'm thinking of. You never lend me anything without a great fuss."

"I thought you two were friends. You've spent a lot of time together. Now it sounds as if you're jealous."

"Well, it's true, isn't it? There's a big difference between the way you treat me and the way you treat him. There's no leeway with me, but your brother can't do anything wrong."

She is willing to think about this.

"He's only here for a while, so I can be indulgent. You're long-term and I have to make boundaries or it won't work. And Tim is family. You can't be so selfish as to think I shouldn't have time for my family."

Again he hears one word above the others – the word 'selfish'. He eats in silence. There's a chance of turning himself around, being reasonable and making peace with her. He would love to get over this unnecessary irritability and make the morning good. He waits for the bad feelings to go away. And against his own will and his expectation he lets out an angry sentence.

"I'm not selfish."

She looks up.

"Or at least not selfish in the way Tim is. He's waited on hand and foot here."

She gets out of bed and walks across the room to get her cigarettes. Her nakedness puts a crowd of thoughts and feelings into his mind. He's aroused, but with it comes something like a memory of last night's dream. He wants sex but something in his head will make sure it can't happen. Much more than this he wants tenderness. He wants it and it can't happen now. She has returned to her bed with a cigarette and an ashtray, a small barricade against him.

"You smoke so much now. And you and your brother get so pissed and stoned all the time."

"And you don't?"

"I try to keep up," he says sadly, "I try, but nothing seems very real when we're like that all the time. I don't like it."

"Okay," she says.

There is a finality in this word. The morning is lost. He sits at the table with an empty cereal bowl in front of him. He feels sorry for himself but he also senses that this is inappropriate.

"I think you should go," she says.

"I suppose I should."

He gets up from the table and collects together a few belongings. Turning before he goes out of the door he manages one conciliatory word.

"Sorry."

Later in the week, Sean has parked his car below the castle and is walking along the prom into town. The sea is on his left-hand side, still, calm and glossy, with a sheen of reflected light over an almost imperceptible swell. There are an unusually large number of small boats dotted over its surface, sailing dinghies trying to catch the small offshore breeze, leisure-craft carrying anglers, a fishing boat loaded with piles of lobster-pots. Through the holiday crowds he catches sight of her brother coming towards him. He is surprisingly pleased. The two men stand and smile at each other.

"I've missed you," the younger man says simply. "I can't really enjoy the seaside if there's no one to share it with."

"Cath and I had a little disagreement."

"I know. At least I can guess. It's alright, it's par for the course. And it makes her paint really well. I think when she's angry she loses her self-consciousness and her work is great." He looks Sean in the eye, "So you are good for her – in one way or another."

They don't know what else to say to each other. Sean is awkward; Tim smiles, unconcerned.

"Coffee?" he says. "I've found a café that has interesting people dropping in. It's almost cosmopolitan. Well, okay it's not like being in the city or anything. But it's the best I've found around here."

In the café Sean feels mildly elevated. It's laughable how little he and Tim have in common – they can hardly sustain a conversation – but he likes being here with the attractive young man. He feels special. There is some sort of emotion attached to being with someone who has his lover's facial expressions and gestures and manner of speaking. And Tim is wearing a blue sweatshirt that belongs to her but which just about fits him.

"Buy her a present," the young man says. "We can go around the shops together. Between us we'll find something she'll like."

So they do the thing that Sean most dislikes and Tim most enjoys. They buy a little book of detachable postcards of pictures by Georgia O'Keefe: city views, deserts, shells, flowers.

"The reproduction is seriously crap but it's something," Tim says. "I still think we should get something more."

In another shop, Tim helps Sean choose a small silver brooch for her. It's expensive but she will like it. Tim decides that the book of postcards will be from him. They can go back together and shower her with presents.

"Can we stop at your place and get your flute and some music?" Tim asks. "I want us to play some music together, the three of us. I've persuaded Cath that she can be creative in more than one direction at a time."

Back at the flat she is happy to see her lover again. And to see him and her brother getting on so well. She is pleased to get presents out of the blue and gives both men a hug and a kiss. Together they play a Handel flute sonata speedily adapted by Tim. She is on electric bass, Sean is on flute, and Tim plays harmonic infill.

Over the next few days they have a good time. She paints and the men go beach-combing. In the evening they drink and smoke dope together. Sometimes they play music. They talk of busking on the sea-front. Tim's collection of necklaces increases. Sometimes in the afternoon, needing a fix of urban life, he goes to town to walk the streets and look in shop windows. Catherine and Sean can spend some of the afternoon making love.

One evening they eat a supper of Mexican food cooked by Tim, the sort of food he most enjoyed in New York and misses in Britain. The food is hot enough to require the drinking of large amounts of cheap lager. Afterwards they go to the pub and carry on drinking. Sean feels good with the food and alcohol inside him, with his lover's head on his shoulder and her arm around his waist. He watches her brother at the bar, his easy charm with people. Tim has an open expression, will smile beautifully at the least provocation, is interested in people, flirts with both sexes, is exhibitionistic in the childlike way that people accept. And he's carefree. Sean knows that this is part of what people find attractive in the man. Carefree, gentle, beautiful, talented and spoilt. He knows that, with Tim, carefree can equal careless often enough – careless with other people's property, certainly. And sometimes it's worse than that, sometimes it equals uncaring, an unwillingness to consider consequences; a perfect, unabashed selfishness. But this is fine for a while. Sean will enjoy playing music, beach-combing, making love in the afternoon, forgetting about his own work. One day the brother will go off somewhere else and things will be normal again.

Later in the evening Tim gets the urge to perform. He squeezes himself in place at the upright piano and plays jazz chords and little lines of melody. After a while he starts singing in a clear fine voice, jazz standards, songs from the repertoires of Nat King Cole and Ella Fitzgerald. He keeps going back to one short song:

Say, it's only a paper moon,
Sailing over a cardboard sea,
But it wouldn't be make-believe
If you believed in me.

He is bought drinks; they collect on top of the piano as he is too busy playing to keep up. Cath goes over from time to time and brings them back for her and Sean – he tackles the beers and she manages the whiskies. She abandons restraint in her drinking tonight. She is happy that her brother is the centre of attention and her lover is by her side. Happy to be able to drink without the unpleasant feeling of spending money she doesn't have.

The front door of the pub is locked, the thick curtains are drawn and the drinking goes on. It is 2am when the three of them leave the pub by the back door and cross the road to her flat. Halfway across the road she stumbles and the two men must catch her before she falls. Then she won't move, she feels sick and they have to hold her steady until it passes. So they stand together there between the two rows of terraced houses that make up the village, holding onto each other, swaying drunkenly. Tim is humming 'It's Only A Paper Moon' quietly to himself, but there is no moon, the sky must have clouded over. The only other sound comes through the alley-ways between the houses: it must be high tide now, the surf is breaking onto the pebbles at the top of the beach.

When they manage to get her upstairs and into the flat she is barely conscious. They take off some of her clothes, lift her onto the bed and cover her with a blanket. She descends immediately into something like sleep. Then the two men sit opposite each other on battered armchairs. Sean opens two cans of beer and gives one to his friend. Tim rolls a joint, lights it and passes it to his sister's lover.

The next morning Sean finds himself standing on the sand at the mouth of the estuary. The tide is coming in fast. All around him the sand-banks are shrinking and breaking up into smaller and smaller islands as the water rises. He moves when the water comes close to his feet. The remaining patches of sand are almost recognisable as the shape of continents, and he finds himself thinking of them as large land-masses, viewed from above, from an aircraft or a spaceship. The world is changing shape beneath him. Tim would like this, he thinks, he liked miniature landscapes, he couldn't see the bigger picture. He left in such a hurry and so determinedly this morning, speaking pleasantly but giving no explanation. Cath said she was used to this happening. But Sean is disconcerted, he knows this subject will become a no-talk zone. He jumps from island to island to avoid getting cut off by the tide. Her brother left very suddenly and he believes that he will get the blame.

TEN

"How can you carry on writing that thing?"

Julian speaks without looking up from his work. He seems cross with me today. I've been enjoying myself but I don't think he is. We've been doing a two man job with the tractor-mounted hoe. He drives the little grey tractor, the wheels either side of a bed of leeks, and behind him I sit on the hoe that sticks out the back. I have a metal seat and a sort of handle-bar to steer. As he drives down the field (it doesn't seem to work very well up hill) I steer the three prongs of the hoe so that they travel between the rows of the crop and lift the weeds up to wilt and dry in the sunshine and wind. It's quicker than hand weeding, but the crop has to be set up correctly and the weather must be good: sunshine and wind to dry out the weeds; rain will settle them back into the soil. The hoe is mounted on the three point linkage, and at the end of a row Julian pulls a lever and the hoe, with me on it, is lifted high off the ground while he drives to the top of the field. Each time we drive back I'm riding high up and I'm able to see over the hedge and across the farmland all around. It's a slow, slightly absurd, pastoral fairground ride. We have spent half the morning driving up and down the field without any opportunity for conversation. I've been concentrating hard on steering the hoe on the way down and enjoying the view on the way up.

Now we've stopped the tractor and must hoe the last rows by hand because the field is too steep here. How can I carry on writing that thing? It's an interesting question. It should be hard but it isn't. Okay, some of what I write is based on memories, but the feelings those memories used to evoke don't arise now. I never visualise her or hear her voice, or imagine the smell or touch of her. She is not a real person to me now. Or is there more to it than this?

We are hoeing weeds out of the dry soil, moving methodically up the slope. The combination of sun and wind make it a perfect temperature for working outdoors, better than the intense heat of high summer. Julian would normally work much faster than me and get way ahead – the fact that we are still working side by side suggests that he is waiting for an answer.

"It shouldn't be possible," I say. "I think some kind of protective barrier comes down. It's simple really. Sometimes it's fragments of memories, distorted memories, but I don't vividly remember the person involved in the events. But mostly it's fiction – perhaps you don't understand that."

"It makes me angry sometimes."

Julian is one of the least angry people I know so this is worrying.

"I'm sorry," I say. "You don't have to read it."

"What annoys me is their selfishness. Loving someone is wanting the best for them even if sometimes it's not good for you. Your lovers don't seem to do that."

"Maybe they love too much."

"What does that mean? Too much? Surely the more deeply you love someone the more you have to give."

I have to concentrate on not accidentally hoeing out the wrong plant when Julian is right next to me; I also have to work fast to keep up with him. So it takes me a time to answer. We are halfway up the field in strong wind so I have to shout my carefully thought out words.

"Maybe it's most selfish when it's most intense," I say. "When you love someone very much you're vulnerable to being hurt. It's dangerous. Self-protection becomes more of a necessity."

"I don't understand it," Julian says. "I want to understand but I don't."

Soon he leaves me in the field to continue alone until lunchtime. This I enjoy very much. I'm beginning to realise that my enjoyment of my surroundings has changed under Julian's influence. I have always liked the countryside, big views, changing weather. But Julian makes me see and hear the detail, particular small wild flowers, certain birds in their place and season. Now, after the silence of summer, there is a little birdsong again but it's muted like a memory. There's a robin singing in the hedge nearby, small snatches of its song coming to me on the wind, memories of spring. The rhythm of my work and the sound of the wind in the trees are therapeutic to me, soothing. But Julian is obviously in a different frame of mind today. Gradually it occurs to me that the unreal person of my fiction corresponds to a very real person in his life. Distance, the distance of time, makes me safe. That's not possible for him. I think of his ideas about love. I know she and I loved more, I just know it. But is it possible that in their cooler relationship they have more space for caring? Usually I keep any thoughts of them out of my mind. There is also something like superiority in my attitude to their relationship. That feeling is being threatened now. But I'm happy up here on the hill even if Julian isn't. Perhaps when I go down for lunch I can cheer him up.

As lunchtime approaches I stop and leave my hoe leaning on the hedge marking the place where I've left off work. I walk down the hill to the farmyard, ready for a rest and something to eat. As I open the gate I see a VW Beetle parked in the yard. I freeze. No it's ridiculous, there are lots of Beetles around and she said that she would never buy another one after the accident. Besides, she never comes here. So I take a deep breath and go to fetch my lunch bag out of the shed. On the way across the yard I look into the back of the car and see an artist's portfolio, a bass guitar and two empty wine bottles. I go hot and cold in an instant. The door of the farmhouse is open and I can hear two voices but I can't make them out. It's her car. This is stupid, I know, but it has a strong effect on me, this person of my imagination and memory coming to life so suddenly. And in a panic I go into the big barn and hide behind the door. I don't know what emotions I'm feeling but I know their physical manifestations. I'm breathing fast, my stomach is churning and my face feels strange, as if all the blood has drained from it. The voices seem to be getting louder. I climb the stepladder that leans against the boat, push it away as if that somehow makes me safer, and climb aboard. I go into the little fo'c'sl cabin and slide the door closed behind me.

So here I am, in a sort of triangular cupboard consisting entirely of a triangular bed that fits into the front of the vessel. This seems symbolic but it's all absurd and laughable. In fact it's more than absurd. It feels very, very unreal. Firstly I'm on the boat – yes I'm on the fucking boat. Outside is a VW Beetle with, in effect, her signature on it – bass guitar, portfolio and wine bottles. Like a cliché out of my story. Fiction and reality are coalescing and this is actually frightening. I sit down cross-legged on the bed (the cabin is too low to stand) and wait for something to happen. I would like to hear the car start up and drive away. Is this a trick Julian's playing on me? Maybe he thought I was trying to change his reality with my fiction and he got in first. But he's really not that sort of person, he wouldn't do that to me. And me, huddled in the fo'c'sl of a boat in some hilltop farmyard. This is ridiculous.

It's not possible for me to sit still in here so I climb out, having checked that the coast is clear. I can still hear voices and the car is still there so I climb into the old hay-loft at the far end of the barn. I'm behaving like a child or a madman. It's pretty dark up here. I don't want to hear the sound of her voice and I don't want to see Julian and her together. But this is stupid, it couldn't be her. But the contents of the car? Surely I imagined those things – they are more like something out of my story than anything real. The voices are definitely getting louder now; they are going to find a frightened lunatic hiding in the hay-loft. Part of me laughs at this but I don't like it one bit. Julian stores old tools up here. I take a big old screwdriver and lever away a rotten board from the back of the barn. The light comes in a little and I've got a view across the fields. I squeeze through the gap in the boards, lower myself down as much as possible, then jump.

Now I'm safe, as if the stuff on the other side of the barn is a bad dream from which I've escaped. I'm leaning against the wall of the barn looking across the countryside spread in front of me. I'm next to the shower that won't be used again this year as the weather is cooling down. I want to laugh out loud at myself. But I'm not going back there. I'll cut across country through Gareth and Olivia's farm and down their lane to the main road. I will try to be a rational person tomorrow; this is neither the time nor the place. Like a fugitive I hurry away from the barn, climb a fence, and head off across the fields.

It is still an invigorating day to be outdoors, and the route I take across the fields has fine views across the countryside. The wind is picking up and it pushes the branches of trees back and forth. I notice that the leaves of the beech trees have already begun to change colour but not one of them is ready to be blown off yet. If the wind continues to increase there will be some storm damage. Part of me is happy and excited. My emotions are stirred. I feel that I've escaped from the pages of my own novel. It's certainly good to be on a hilltop and not hiding in a boat. I have lots of energy and actually run across the fields in the wind.

Of course, all of the dogs in Gareth's farmyard start barking when I try to pass through, and Olivia comes out.

"What are you doing here John?" she asks, giving me a curious look. I'm breathing hard from running and my face must show my agitation.

"Do you want a cup of tea?"

"Yes," I say, trying to return to some semblance of normality. "That would be very good."

She leads me into the house.

"You look like you've seen a ghost," she says.

I have to use the toilet and I look at my face in the mirror while I'm in there. I do look like I've seen a ghost. I look shaken. But there's also an inane smile on my face that I'm surprised to see. There's a momentarily younger and happier person than the one I usually see looking back at me. I go into the kitchen where Olivia is standing near the kettle. I can't make any attempt at explanation to her but I'm pleased to be here. I feel like I'm with an older sister. She's very calming and kind. I sit at the kitchen table and she gives me tea and cake.

"Have you had a haircut?" she asks. "You look younger."

"No. I think it must be the wind."

"How's the novel?"

"It's going very well. Actually too well."

"How's that?"

"It's getting itself mixed up with reality."

Olivia looks knowingly at me.

"Surely there's a lot of reality going into it isn't there?"

"It's not reality getting into the novel but the novel escaping from the pages and into the real world. That's what's troubling me."

Olivia can't understand this. She looks quizzically at me but I don't want to explain. There's a long silence. Then she motions for me to look out of the window.

"The cows are all standing by the gate, do you see?"

"Don't they always do that?"

"They do it if they're short of grass or bothered by flies in hot weather. Today they want to escape the wind."

"But it's just as windy in the next field."

"They do it anyway. They're just as irrational as people."

"Do we do that?" I say, wondering if maybe this has some bearing on my behaviour.

"Gareth did it all the time when he was young. I don't think he would mind me telling you. He used to keep moving from place to place to escape his troubles. He calls it 'doing a geographical'. He showed me that cows do the same thing."

She looks pleased with herself, "It's a kind of metaphor, isn't it? You could use it in your writing."

"This writing thing has really stuck to me, hasn't it?" I say.

"You have to remember that we don't meet a great many creative people out here. You're a curiosity to us."

I drink my tea and muse on the power of fiction. There's no

escaping it.

"I would like you to let me read some of your work someday," she says.

"I'll consider it. But people won't accept fiction. They look for autobiography all the time and find it even when it's not there. So it's difficult to show it to people you know. And I'm sure it's not very good so that makes it potentially very embarrassing. Letting you read it would be like taking my clothes off in front of you."

This makes Olivia smile. She's looking at me teasingly, amused. "Now that you mention it," she says. I think I must be looking terrified because she bursts into laughter and is still laughing when Julian walks in. He looks very serious. "I'm looking for Gareth," he says and then sees me sitting there.

"John was just about to take his clothes off," Olivia says, "but never mind."

I give a resigned smile and Julian smiles back at me, "What are you doing here? No it's alright, I understand." I feel stupid.

"It's Wednesday," says Olivia, "Gareth's at market all day. I'm sorry"

Julian is concerned and agitated about something.

"Will you have some tea?" Olivia asks.

"No, I need to get back on. Do you want a lift back John? It's safe now."

Julian and I drive back in his Land Rover. "I honestly had no idea that she was coming," Julian says, and we are silent for the rest of the journey. Today has been disturbing for me. Perhaps I can get my lunch bag from the shed, eat a little, and then get back onto the land for a couple of hours and try to make sense of today's events. But it begins to rain; perhaps it will be a shower or maybe something more. We drive into Julian's farmyard which looks different to me now.

"I don't suppose you've had any lunch," Julian says. "Do you want to come indoors for a while?"

So we sit in the kitchen and listen to the wind and rain outside, both aware of the absence of that other person who was here earlier. It's cooler weather than it has been for a long time and I give a shiver. When we have eaten I want to get away but the rain continues outside and it seems impolite to sit there in silence.

"What did you want Gareth for?" I ask.

"Gareth?" Julian says, roused from his silence, "Oh it's nothing. It can wait for another day." He looks worried and unhappy.

In front of me on the table there are some letters, Julian's morning post still unopened.

"Your initials are JS, like the composer," I say. "What does the S stand for?"

"It's an old family name, I have some Irish forebears."

"So it's not Sebastian then?"

"No."

"Aren't you going to tell me what it is?"

"JS is Julian Sean."

"Sean. That's an interesting name. Isn't that the name you suggested for a certain fictional character of mine?"

"Yes, it is. It's a good name."

I'm bemused. It's been a long day. It's all too much to take in. I wish it would stop raining and I could get outside again. I need to think.

"I would love to get to the end of your piece of writing," Julian says.

"Why?"

"I want to know if it's finished or did it just end."

"What does that mean?" I ask.

"I mean I want to know if the relationship came to a complete, never-to-be-repeated end point. Two people who have finished loving each other. Or two people who still love but it can't carry on. Or something else again."

This is exactly the wrong time to ask me this question.

"I don't know," I say, "I don't know how many more chapters I'll write or how I'll finish it."

"I think you do know," Julian says, almost angry with me. "Also I'm getting impatient. It takes a week or two before you're ready to give me another little scene of the two of you, and I really want to get to the end of it. To understand what happened."

"This is a crazy conversation. You make it sound like I'm writing a true story about real people and real events. Of course there are bits of my own experience embedded in it. But that's all. It's fiction, fiction, fiction. I can't tell you the end until I've written it. You're talking like it's all in the past and I've just got to regurgitate it. Actually it's in the future – I haven't written it yet. The story hasn't happened until I write it down."

"But it's about her isn't it?"

"Yes and no. Definitely plenty of no."

The rain has stopped outside but it is still cool and gloomy in the kitchen. Perhaps the sun will come out later in the day. Julian has one more question to ask me.

"Do you think you will want to see her again one day? In the future?"

I shake my head, "How many times does one man jump off the same cliff?"

ELEVEN

The day will be over soon and Sean needs to be outdoors, preferably by the sea. The road from the door of his house leads to her house, that is the way the world is constructed for him. She still lives in the village that stretches along a road between the marshes and the sea and he finds himself driving there even though she will be busy working and won't want to see him until tomorrow afternoon. He drives the length of the village, parks by the concrete embankment that keeps back the sea, and will walk on the beach until sunset. But there is no beach. It is one of those times of year when there is a great tidal range, with very low and very high tides. Now it is as high as he has ever seen it, completely covering the sand and coming close to the top of the shingle ridge. The sea is very still under a gentle offshore breeze. The sun in the west has disappeared behind a bank of cloud and there will be little in the way of a sunset. The light is very clear and, from the top of the embankment, he can see the whole curve of the bay, headlands and hills stretching away from him in both directions. The bay this evening is an overfilled cup, the sea calmly threatening the lowland.

But it gives him an excuse for calling in, he went to the beach but it was underwater. He walks to her house and rings the doorbell. The house is quiet, the bottom two storeys are unoccupied at this time of year. At the top of the house Catherine will be working in the large attic space, he can go away again if he's disturbing her. He rings again. He wants to see her now, and not knowing whether she is in or not unnerves him. He goes through an alley-way between the houses and onto the beach. He can't see her skylight window from here; the house is in darkness and she must be out. He sits on the little strip of stones that remain above water and watches the sea. The backs of the houses here are well protected, some have wooden or metal shutters for their lower windows. The little concrete backyards are guarded by low walls and instead of gates have openings filled by removable slotted timbers. All are in place except hers – she must have been dragging in some preposterous lump of driftwood again. He gets up and puts the timbers in place to stop any possibility of flooding. Imagine a sea as high as this and a storm at the same time. It must happen very rarely.

He is increasingly uncomfortable on the beach and gets up to go. He wishes she wanted his company as much as he wants hers. Then he hears music coming from her room. The sea is very still and quiet and he can recognise the sound of an album he has heard many times before. But he has rung the doorbell twice and there's nothing more to do. He makes his way back to the car and drives away. The music continues to sound in his head, a jazz sax compilation that she would put on in the early days to cover the sound of their noisy love-making. She never played the record at other times. As he drives through the village and up the hill towards home the record is still playing. He is alone in the car and the record is playing in her room. He feels very bad and can't sleep for the first part of the night. He gets up and re-reads some of her old letters to him:

> *And if we did split up one day? I honestly can't imagine there ever being anyone else. What would be the point? There is no one else out there who I could be connected to in the way I'm connected to you.*

It helps him to sleep.

In the morning he wakes late and lies in bed with mixed emotions. He arrives at the beach to find the tide going out very fast, leaving a great expanse of shining wet sand below the shingle ridge. The sea surprises. It leaves different things on the beach on different days, today a line of small delicate razor shells along the sand, not one of them damaged. In among them are tiny spherical jellyfish – sea gooseberries. He crouches down and investigates the stranded creatures. Then he moves on, drawn to her house even though she doesn't expect to see him until the afternoon. He sits on the stones at the back, a few hours early, maybe taking some sort of chance. He knows that she might come out and he can imagine her first words, 'What are you doing hanging around out here?' Perhaps he should come back later. But he hears a low whistle behind him and turns. Catherine is in scruffy paint-splattered clothes, her hair fixed back in two untidy plaits. She is particularly beautiful to him. She walks carefully barefoot across the pebbles to him and smiles.

"I dreamt of you so much, and this morning I went to the phone box and tried to call you. And here you are."

He doesn't speak but only smiles.

"Come in, come and see the lonely artist and her work. Can you bear to be indoors, away from the sea?"

He smiles, shrugs and nods. Speechless, happy. Up in her attic she shows him a huge canvas of distorted people, half-covered by black and flecks of silver.

"I came out late last night," she says. "The sea was very high but going out. The moon had come up. It was very still and eerie. And when I went back indoors I took this painting that I've spent days on and inundated it with black paint. Brave aren't I? Then I dreamt of you."

She is excited and fulfilled, her eyes very warm on him.

"And here you are," she says again. "What did you dream of?"

"Mermaids," he says. "Silent mermaids watching me from a distance, laughing and talking together. But not talking to me. If I went towards them they would drop below the water and reappear further away. Maybe they were you."

"Poor you. You should have been here, I wouldn't disappear under the waves."

"I should have been," he says.

She stands close, turns sideways a little and then rests herself lightly against him, one leg lifted so that the tips of her toes are on the floor. She looks at him out of the corner of her eyes and touches his lower lip with one finger. He knows this set of movements that she sometimes makes. It is her unselfconscious unspoken, 'shall we?' It is the most tender thing he has ever experienced. He makes appreciative noises and she kisses the side of his neck. 'We shall,' he thinks.

And now it is early afternoon and they haven't left the house. They have made love, talked about their dreams, made plans to play music together again and watched a soft drizzle form droplets on the skylight. She has switched on a little glowing electric fire. The room is warm and they are sitting on the sofa half-clothed. She wears his T-shirt and below it a long thin cotton sarong. He wears only his old jeans. Only when they're together can they be like this.

"We made love in the mid-morning," he says. "Only lovers do that."

"Yes... that's true," she says, the tone of her voice asking why he's stating the obvious.

"What I mean is, people make love at night, or in the morning when they wake up, or on a summer's afternoon. But people don't make love at eleven o'clock in the morning. It just isn't done."

"But we do."

"We're special. That's what I'm saying."

She rises and makes tea for them both. He watches the movement of her limbs beneath the thin cotton. Then she sits and begins to roll a joint.

"I bought some dope, do you want some?" she says. "It's going to rain all day and we can't go anywhere."

"You know it's early in the day for me. I don't know why but I just don't want to get stoned or drunk until the evening."

"It's because you're uptight and want to be in control," she says.

"Go on then. I'll be different today. I don't mind."

They sit smoking and drinking their tea. The room is warm and he climbs onto the table to open the skylight a little. The sea is a way out, invisible through the drizzle.

"You know it's part of the creative process," she says.

"What is?"

"Letting go."

"You mean getting drunk or stoned at all hours?"

"Not being uptight about it, I mean. It's like you disapprove of me sometimes. It's not fair that you should judge me."

"I don't disapprove of you now," he says, smiling.

He looks across the room at a stack of old fish-boxes she has collected off the beach. They are made of brightly coloured plastic, red, blue, yellow and green, but old, distressed by the action of the sea. They bear the name of the boat they belong to or the name of its owner.

"Do you think Cecil Sharkey has met Angel Emiel?" he asks.

She looks across at the boxes. "I've often wondered about that. What do you think? Are they friends or enemies?"

"I think they're rivals in love," he says. " And I bet she ends up with Mr Sharkey and not poor old Angel. It's always the way."

"I think Angel has run off with the mermaids," she says.

They have finished their tea and are sitting close beside each other on the old sofa. Her legs are half curled together, under the blue sarong, her feet sticking out at the bottom, one resting on the other.

"You could be a mermaid," he says.

"Oh yeah."

"No, you really could. With your legs curled up like that and your feet together. I can't tell from here."

She smiles indulgently at him, "You are a bit stoned, aren't you?"

He kneels beside her and runs his hands from her hips, down along the outside of her thighs and calves to her feet.

"You might be a mermaid," he says with a cheeky grin. Her

feet are cold and he rubs them between his hands to warm them. He kisses the tops of her toes.

"It's hard to tell," he says, repeating his actions.

"You're ridiculous. And I'm very happy to be human."

She draws him up to her and spreads her limbs around him.

"Let's be human," she says. And they are human for part of the warm drizzly afternoon.

Later they are stretched out at opposite ends of the bath, their legs companionable under the soapy water.

"We don't do much of the slow caresses and tenderness bit. We're manic lovers," she says.

"But it's what you want to do, isn't it?"

"Oh yes."

"And when we make love it seems that it's about expressing what I feel for you. That's what comes first, not hornyness"

"It's the same for me," she says. "That's why it's so good."

"It's not that there's no tenderness. It's just that it's intensified, manic tenderness if you like. Is that right? Is that how it is?"

She looks at him being serious at his end of the bath. She smiles and nods her head enthusiastically, "That's how it is."

They stretch out in the water, rubbing their legs together. He is deep in thought for a moment.

"There's maybe a reason that it's still like this after so long – I mean, more than a year and we're still very passionate in the same way. It's because it's actually so difficult a lot of the time. So it's like constant separations and reunions."

He chooses his words very carefully and looks at her to see what effect they are having.

"And it will be a long time before we are an ordinary couple, some passion spent, ordinary everyday tenderness remaining."

He liked the sound of the word 'everyday'.

She has listened carefully. "I don't do *ordinary*," she says, "I don't think I'm ready for that yet."

Since that last very high tide Sean has bought a set of tide-tables and is learning about the variations in the moon's effect on the sea. He understands that around full moon and new moon the tidal range is at its greatest. At some times of year this is for some reason increased. Tonight, 24 hours after a new moon, there will be the highest tide of the year. Also the weather has changed, westerly winds pushing the sea violently against the land, the waves building up as it continues over many days. She has no phone so he can't contact her to remind her to put the wooden barrier in its place in the back wall of the yard. He imagines the sea flooding into the bottom of her house and the image won't leave his mind. He drives to the end of the village and walks along the beach in the fading light.

The sea is mucky. Heavy rain has filled the rivers that flow into the bay; mud, peat from the hills, branches of riverside trees and the occasional drowned sheep are all flooding down into the sea. The waves are a yellow-grey colour and the high strand-line of the beach is littered with debris of both land and sea. The leaves of oak and ash trees, brought down early by wind and rain, are mixed with seaweed scoured up from the seabed, and they lie together in smelly piles. Plastic fish-boxes that have been submerged long enough to acquire a cover of seaweed and goose barnacles are brought to the shore alongside old fertiliser sacks and fence-posts from farms inland. The beach stinks and the sea writhes under the wind. The waves are riotous and throw themselves at the land in broken rhythms.

He arrives at her place to find the wooden barrier in place after all. He wants company and goes around to the front of her house and rings the doorbell. No answer, of course. He walks down towards the pub in the middle of the village as a heavy rain begins to fall. It is that time of day when curtains are still undrawn and he has glimpses into warm well-lit homes. There is a great contrast between the comfortable indoors and the grim uninhabitable outdoor world. At the pub he looks in through the window, unsure whether to go in or go home. A small group of people around a table look animated and flushed enough to be drunk although it's early in the evening. He recognises some of them but doesn't feel like joining in. A burly man with a great deal of frizzy hair has stood up and left the table. Catherine is visible on the other side, a bottle of beer in her hand. He watches and means to go in but he would feel painfully sober and out of place in the company of these people. He doesn't know if she would want him there. This hurts. He sees her laugh and stand up, perhaps to buy more drinks for everyone. She is unsteady on her feet, from the drink or the shared hilarity, and her hand rests on the shoulder of the man next to her for a moment. He turns from the window and walks back down the street in the rain. The tarmac glistens under the street-lights. Curtains are being drawn against the wet and cold. In the short time that he has been outdoors it has become almost dark and the wind is getting stronger. He looks at the sea before getting into his car. Irregular patches and streaks of foam show in the stray light from the village.

At home, a few miles from the coast, he can hear the wind in the trees, a backdrop of noise and sudden gusts forcing the branches and tearing at the leaves. It is also raining very heavily. He looks at the little booklet of tide-tables and thinks of how high the sea was when he saw it at the last really big tide. In less than two hours the sea will be at its highest all year and she will be very drunk. He sits in an armchair for a long while, his feet curled under him, listening to the wind getting stronger. After an hour he gets up, puts on boots and waterproofs, and sets off again for the village. He drives very slowly and carefully. In some places the road is flooded with water coming down off the hills. In other places he has to get out to clear wind-blown debris from his way: a branch, a dustbin, part of somebody's fence. Before the bend where it enters the village the road is at its lowest point and comes close to the stony beach. His headlights show the road disappearing under a rush of seawater and he pulls over to one side and gets out. Without the car headlights he can see very little at first, his strongest impressions are of the noise of wind and waves. He can see lights on in the village and the reflection of a blue flashing light further down the road. Ahead of him a huge wave crashes over the shingle ridge, increasing the flood across the road. He wades through the cold water as it ebbs.

Here, before the road bends and passes through the village, he is walking towards the sea. When big waves crash over the stones he feels that he is actually below sea level. The wind hits him in gusts and forces him to lean hard enough into it so that when it subsides for a moment he falls to his knees. The second time this happens he remains in that position and looks around him. He is on the outskirts of the village. The sea is hurling itself at the beach and flooding onto the land. Shingle and some big pebbles are being thrown onto the road and against buildings and parked cars. The force of the wind shakes a garden shed as if it is made of jelly and then peels off the roof and takes it away into the darkness, followed by the four walls and much of its contents. Somehow, this is a stimulating and beautiful sight to him. The noise, the force of the wind, the strange sight of ordinary things taking to the air, all this makes him feel light-headed and exhilarated. A small plastic dinghy has been lifted from somewhere and come to rest on the flooded road. Then it is driven by water and wind into the space recently vacated by the garden shed. He laughs out loud like a drunk. Then he remembers that he has come here to find her and see that she is safe. He gets off his knees and staggers into the village, bending forwards and leaning sideways into the wind as he walks.

He has to struggle along the road between the houses to her end of the village. On the landward side of the road the houses are brightly lit and people are looking out of upstairs windows. On the seaward side, her side of the road, houses are dark, the electricity having failed. Some houses have their front doors propped open to let out the sea-water that has come in through doors and windows at the back. It flows out onto doorsteps and into the road in a steady stream. Where there is an alley-way between the houses the sea gushes out onto the road and deposits pebbles, seaweed and plastic bottles. Here between the houses the wind is unpredictable. He stops to watch the improbable phenomenon of water spouting from the top of a down-pipe. A roof-tile is lifted off and hits the road in front of him. The wind gets a purchase and lifts more tiles off the roof, each one blown upwards at first and then sliding down the roof to crash onto the street.

Further along the road are a fire-engine and an ambulance parked next to a crashed car. There's no one in the car now and the firemen look out of their cab window through the rain. He continues down the street very alert to the possibility of falling tiles. Each time he passes an alley-way between the seaward houses he struggles through gushing water and debris. One powerful flow washes him off his feet. He sees people watching him from a window and waves to indicate that he is alright. In an absurd way he is enjoying himself. The noise is overwhelming. It is every waterfall, mountain stream, stormy beach, express train and motorway junction he has heard in his life all rolled into one cacophony. The biggest waves seem to shake the village, the noise echoes back and forth between the houses. Near her house things seem worse, with some front doors forced open by the pressure of water from behind.

And now he reaches her house. The front door is intact and the house is in darkness. She may be inside. He realises that he is uselessly shouting her name even though he himself can't hear his voice above the uproar. He decides to get into the house from the back and starts up one of the narrow alley-ways. Halfway along he can see a large wave breaking above the stony beach. He braces himself but it hits him and washes him out into the street. He is soaked to the skin and has seaweed clinging to his arms. He makes another attempt, knowing that it is stupid and dangerous, but elated by his battle with the elements. He is shouting her name again for no reason. He feels purposeful and intensely alive. He reaches the back of the houses and rests against a wall. The sea level here is below that of the shingle ridge but each wave comes over, hurling stones at the houses and at him. He waits for what might be a gap in the waves and rushes along the stones and in through her open back door. He wades through the water in the hall and goes up two flights of stairs to the attic. He pushes her door open.

Here at the top of the house the sound of the storm is softened and in the dark there is a stillness. He can't see if she is there. He has no torch, he is soaked to the bone and begins to feel foolish. He feels his way into her bathroom, strips off and dries himself with a towel. He sits on the toilet while deciding what to do next. Of course. She likes candlelight when she is in the bath. He searches with his fingers and finds a candle and cigarette-lighter on the shelf. He lights a candle and with a towel around his waist he makes his way to her room and finds her curled up asleep under the duvet, oblivious to the storm outside. He looks at his watch. High tide was an hour ago and now the tide will begin to go out quickly. The sea will do no more than it has already done. He gets carefully into bed beside her and begins to get warm again. She sleeps soundly beside him, breathing regularly, smelling a little of drink and cigarette smoke. He lies awake for some time, listening to the sound of the storm and wondering what he is doing there.

When the room lightens in the morning he opens his eyes to find her awake beside him. It sounds as if the wind has abated and the sea is a long way out across the sand. She props herself on one arm and smiles good-naturedly at the man she has found in her bed. She says one word: "Why?"

TWELVE

The sea is a constant restless backdrop of sound. Wave after wave breaking in the open sea, breaking against the land. He is in trouble in the water and as the night progresses the sea-noise increases and his struggle intensifies. He is striving to reach the mermaid who would save him if she could see him. He raises one arm and shouts to her but can't be heard. She drops below the waves and reappears further away. For a long time he tries to get closer to her, to make her notice him. The other side of the window, raindrops running down the pane, she raises a beer bottle, drinks, and smiles at her friends. He hears loud pub-music mixed with the sound of sea, wind and rain. He calls her name but can't hear the sound of his own voice. He is too hot and pushes the bedclothes away to let the cool night air onto his sweat-covered skin. She is dancing with a man he recognises but can't name, she rubs herself against this man and looks into his eyes. The sea is louder now and he must put in place all the boards that protect the land from flooding. The waves are throwing pebbles up to the top of the beach, angrily rearranging the shoreline. His task is endless. He repeats the same motion, lifting the wooden barriers into place again and again. He is cold, pulls the covers around him, curls up and shivers. Only towards morning does the sea-noise diminish and his struggle cease.

Sean wakes late in the day, calm now but also invigorated. In some way he overcame the forces against him in the night. He lies still in his bed and watches the patterns made on the wall by sunlight coming through the ash trees outside his window. He feels like a hero, triumphant and weary. He went to her in the storm and saved her from the sea and that is why he is ill now and has been feverish and delirious all night. He gets out of bed feeling good about being awake and alive in daylight. He is surprised by how pale and ill he looks in the mirror, but ignores this and goes down to the kitchen for tea and toast. The air outside is still and the sun looks warm. He goes out to walk around his woodland garden and down the lane a little. Then, exhausted, he goes back indoors, undresses and gets back into bed to sleep again.

There are two nights of troubled sleep and two days of feeble inactivity. His dreams tell him that he has done something heroic and a feeling of exultancy is carried into his daytime conscious-ness. He went to her house in the storm, that was it. Only at the end of the second day of illness does he begin to feel bored, wishing that she would come to him. He would like to wake tomorrow with her in bed beside him. But then he imagines her as she was in the morning after the storm, looking across at him and asking 'why?' This 'why' undermines his other feelings.

The next day he is lonely, irritated by her failure to visit him. When she finally arrives he acts as if she is unwelcome. He cooks lunch for the two of them but feels that he is the poor recovering invalid and that she should be looking after him. She stays an hour and then leaves without kissing him because she doesn't want to catch his 'flu. He won't be able to work for a few days, he can't contact her because she has no phone, and he is lonely. That was the first time that they had been in each other's company without touching. At one time, he remembers, to be together without making love was rare enough to be a novelty.

A few days later he drives down to the village to walk on the beach and to see her. He has been sleeping until midday, his sense of time is skewed and he is surprised to find that, after a short time, the sun is low on the horizon. It seems to him that it is setting halfway through the afternoon. It is ominous and unsettling. The sea is a long way out and the beach is vast and deserted. He is still weak from being ill and sits on the stones looking out across the expanse of shining wet sand. Then he walks slowly towards the sea and the setting sun. The clouds are long parallel stripes of orange and lurid pink stretched above the horizon. In between appears the sky, green close to the sea and then many shades of blue, gradually darkening higher up. These bizarre other-worldly colours are reflected by the wet sand in front of him. He walks unsteadily on through this unearthly scene – strange sky above and below him, a metallic glistening sea ahead. A flock of gulls flies across his view – creatures of the water and air; there is nothing here of the land. He reaches the sea, stands and watches. The colours remain for a while after the sunset then quickly fade to grey. He turns and walks along the beach to the village.

She is happy when he arrives and leads him to the attic. There she shows him a large canvas on which garish streaks of colour have been applied with a palette knife. A narrow strip of grey bisects the picture horizontally. Above and below are mirror images of bold wild colours. She stands excitedly to one side of the half-made picture. Then she rushes forward to him and gives him a kiss and a warm hug.

"I've got to carry on right now. You make tea, sit down and be invisible for half an hour. After that I'm all yours."

She moves back to the picture and rearranges tubes of paint on the small table beside it. Then she turns to him again, "You were on the beach too, weren't you? Are you well again now? Half an hour, I promise."

He doesn't have time to speak before she turns, picks up a palette knife and begins to apply more colour to the canvas. Her excitement changes to focussed concentration and she moves in a way that he has not seen before. There is something feline and predatory about her movement. He does as she says and makes himself inconspicuous but it doesn't seem necessary as she soon becomes totally absorbed in her work to the exclusion of anything in her surroundings. He wants her to finish and make love to him. There was something sexual about her excitement when he came in and now she is beautiful in the intensity of her work.

More and more paint goes on. The stripes of colour are curved, as if she looked at the scene through a fish-eye lens. The picture depicts the moment after sunset; it seems as if the sky has curved about a point that marks the sun's absence.

His thoughts wander as he waits for her to finish; half an hour was a while ago. He has time to start being resentful towards her. Her idea of a relationship doesn't seem to include looking after someone when they are ill. In this same space he took care of her after the car accident, and when he came to her in the storm it was because he was worried about her safety. So when she finally stops work he says nothing positive about her picture, nothing about how beautiful she looks to him as she works, and nothing of their simultaneous experience of the sunset.

"You can't capture it really, can you?" he says. "It's a complete sensory experience. It's sound, the wind on your face, the changing of the colours with time, the whole sky wrapped right around you. To me it would be futile to try to capture it."

Part of him thinks that the painting is wonderful – just as the person who painted is wonderful. He fails to say this.

"How are you now?" she asks. "Have you been ill for days? Poor you."

"I'm alright now but it's cold in here."

She switches on the electric fire and makes him more tea. She is kind and attentive but his resentment won't go away.

"I wish you had visited me more in the last few days," he says.

"No harm in wishing."

"What have you been doing?" he asks.

"Working of course. I'm an artist you know. I have things to do. Things that are important to me. I'm willing to be selfish on occasion."

"On occasion!"

"And you're never selfish? she asks. "You never put yourself first? Get real please."

He sits on the sofa and sulks. He doesn't want this to be happening. She distracts herself by tidying the room and he watches her. They both need to smoulder on for a while and then cool down. He sees the beauty in her movements about the room. Resentment and anger begin to fade away.

"I'm sorry," he says, with a smile that communicates some of those other things he should be saying to her. She crosses the room to him.

"Poor you. You've gone all pale and thin in the last few days. What can I do to build you up again?"

She kneels in front of him and looks at him with concern.

"Are you still cold?" she asks. Then she stands, takes his hands and pulls him upright. She hugs him and rubs her hands vigorously up and down his back. Then she kisses him on the mouth and rubs up against him.

"Are you warming up?"

They stand together and move their bodies against each other as if for warmth. Their movements gradually become more sexual.

"We would be warm together under your duvet," he says.

She pushes her hand up under his shirt and across his stomach.

"Nothing here," she says. "Your stomach feels all flat and empty. You're not the man I once knew," she smiles. "Come on, lets go to the pub and get you some food. I'll treat you. You need building up."

In the pub she buys beer, cigarettes and a pizza for them to share. He can't eat much and has little stomach for beer either. Some of her local friends arrive and join them, a mixture of half-employed creative types. But it's good, he likes sitting there with her resting against him, he warms to the people around him as the small amount of beer he drinks begins to take effect. He wants to talk about the storm and his strange dreams afterwards, but no one seems to want to hear about it.

"We're all stormed out," she says in explanation. "We've all talked about the storm for days now and it's grown to be old news."

But the man opposite has brought from his pocket a piece of today's newspaper and reads it out loud. A government spokesman has said that global warming will make it necessary to abandon some low-lying areas, even certain villages in remote places, to the sea. They are all delighted that they are living on the edge. It fits in with their bohemian view of themselves. They decide that they'd better drink as much as they can while the pub is still above-water. He can't keep up with them. He feels tired and shaky but isn't getting drunk as they all are. She is at his side, which is good, except that all her talk is directed at her friends. He subsides into silence. When she buys an expensive round of drinks he thinks of the money she owes him. Eventually he decides to go. She follows him to the door.

"Will you get into my bed and keep a place warm for me?" she says. "I'll be with you later. And do say goodbye to my friends."

He waves to them but they don't see him. He can hear the end of a sentence – "... in the Old Submariner..." – followed by loud laughter.

"I'll come to you later," she says, and turns quickly away from him.

He lies awake in her bed for a long while. One man in the pub was often looking across at the two of them. There was something in his expression that sticks in his mind now, a look of some sort of superiority, a sneer. When midnight has passed and the pub should have shut he begins to wonder where she is, who she is with now. He remembers the way the man looked at him.

He is sound asleep when she comes in but is woken by the noise of her knocking something over in the room. Then she is naked beside him. She smells very strongly of alcohol and cigarettes. She runs her hands over his body, down his back and around his buttocks. Then she starts to kiss him and rub herself against him. But she is very drunk and her movements are awkward and clumsy. She raises herself to kiss him and manages to put all her weight onto her elbow, pinching his forearm. He angrily moves away to the far edge of the bed. They are still and quiet for a while and he feigns sleep. Later, he can hear her masturbating. After a while she appears to have given up; lying on her back, she falls into a deep, drunken sleep, snoring loudly. He lies awake, next to the person he loves, but disconnected, lonely.

In the morning he wakes late. She is across the room working on her new painting. She paints over some of yesterday's work. At first he can see a patchwork, a canvas covered by small oblong areas of colour. But something about the changing angles of these blocks takes the eye into the centre of the painting. It is not a flat picture but rather something three-dimensional, that draws you into a depth at the centre, a vortex. It is unsettling to him.

She senses that he is awake.

"Hello unlover," she says sadly.

He doesn't disturb her work but eats a little breakfast and goes out onto the beach without speaking. He walks a little. After the very high tide of the storm he's amazed at how far from the land the sea can sometimes be here. Again there is a large expanse of sand and again there is something remarkable to surprise him. The sea has generated patches of foam that are being pushed up onto the beach by the waves. There the onshore breeze moves the foam up and along the smooth wet sand, smaller patches coalescing into larger blocks as they go. The wet sand reflects the clear blue of the sky making the foam look like so many clouds that have fallen to earth. Where he lives, a little way inland, the seasons progress steadily and predictably through the year, clothing and unclothing the trees and colouring them according to plan. Here, by the sea, things are different every day, as if time itself were chaotic, ragged and uncertain. What would it be like to live here, at the sea's edge?

He goes into the village and buys some bread for her. There's an advert for a house to rent at the other edge of the village by the cliffs. It's bigger and more expensive than where he lives now so he would have to find someone to share it with. Perhaps it could be an answer to the problems between them. To be independent but in the same house with lots of space. He goes to her house but sits out the back on the stones overlooking the sea. He wonders when he should bring up this new idea. He thinks of living by the sea, always on the edge of change, away from the certainties of season. He struggles to remember a particular line of poetry about season and time. Is it about the seaside?

When he goes back up to her room she has stopped working and is tidying brushes and tubes of paint. In this one area of her life she is orderly.

"Love, all alike, no season knows or clime, or hours, days, months, which are the rags of time. And I've bought you a loaf of bread," he says.

"Time is an issue today as it happens. I've got someone coming round to help me make up some picture-frames this afternoon."

"Are you asking me to go?"

"All I'm saying is I'm pretty tied up today. I'm sorry."

"Who's coming round?"

"It's Greg, he was in the pub, but you probably didn't notice him, he's very shy."

He wishes she had taken notice of his line of poetry. In fact her lack of interest in him stands in contrast to those words. He watches her tidying and turns things over in his mind.

"I wish you had some sense of commitment to this relationship," he says.

She stops what she is doing. "I am *committed*, as you put it, to this relationship. But I have other things in my life that are important to me, other people sometimes. I can't just drop everything for you."

"I'm thinking of moving down here to the village. Is it a good idea?"

She looks uncertain and says nothing.

"There's a house for rent but it's too big. I need to share it with someone. I think we could be independent and come and go as we please, but we would always be there for each other." As he speaks the whole thing sounds unworkable. He knows what her answer will be and is angry in advance.

"No way."

"Why?"

"I need space."

"It's a big house."

"Space from you."

She didn't even pause before she said it. Something inside him wants to make this worse.

"Why space from me?" he says.

"This is why. What's happening this very minute. The pressure you put on me. It's possessive. Anything we have will end if you keep doing this to me. Why do you keep doing this?"

"Why space from me? What do you want to do when I'm not around that you can't do when I'm here?"

"I've answered you and you go on and on. All I want to do is my art and not have pointless rows like this one."

"What else do you do?" There is a thought that he won't allow to the front of his mind so he goes on asking questions. He is pushing her into anger. She turns away, her body very tense. When she turns back and looks at him her eyes are narrow and hard. He feels that she will say something cruel or spiteful that may or may not be the truth. Or perhaps she is close to violence.

"Go away."

She has the self-control to say just those two words. He has to do as she asks and turns towards the door. As he goes out he walks past the painting she has just been working on. He wants to get quietly away but another part of him wants to do something hurtful. It doesn't look much like an accident when his shoulder brushes against the painting and knocks it from the easel.

The next day he is reading:

There is hope for us. I need two things – first a big apology for

how you were yesterday. For damaging my painting. Also a break. I think a month. Respect me in this. Is it always jealousy that does this? Because Greg was coming round to help me? He couldn't make it, he has two small children, his partner works, and he couldn't get a babysitter. So don't be jealous of me with him. Jealousy is really your problem – if it ends us it's your fault. Except that perhaps it's too late.
Catherine.

He knows that he has behaved badly. It's easy to write a letter of apology. And now, faced with a month's separation, what he writes is a long love-letter, pages of feelings and memories and hopes for the future. Her reply is as short as it could be, just thank you and a date four weeks from the present, and love. In the past he never doubted that they felt the same about each other. It was true. Now he doesn't know. So his main occupation is to count the days, hope she will change her mind and show her need for him before the month is up. When he goes to bed at night he sees her face before him. When he hears footsteps on the path to his door he immediately believes it is her, coming to visit him. Sometimes he catches a scent of her, as if she is standing close by.

After two weeks without contact he is suspicious. Twice, he stands outside the pub in the dark, watching her through the window. He has not seen her as drunk as this before. She looks unhappy, dependent on the people around her. The *men* around her. He watches a third time and sees her, laughing sadly, leaning back affectionately against the man beside her. He goes to the beach and stands where he believes he will able to see the light from her skylight window when she finally comes home. It is a moonless dark night, the boundary of the sea and land indistinct enough for him to get his feet soaked by an encroaching wave. He watches for what seems like a long time and only goes home when he is too cold to stay any longer.

He wakes at dawn with an image in his mind of her in the pub, resting herself against the man at her side. He returns to the village. There is a thick mist coming in off the sea, wrapping itself around buildings, deadening all sound. He goes across the stones to the back of her house, forces a window and climbs her stairs quietly without his shoes. The door of her room is open and in the pale light he can see her empty bed. He leaves the silent house and drives home slowly through the thickening mist. There he has a painful morning. It seems to him that the worst thing is the not knowing. In the early afternoon he returns to the seaside. He parks some miles away at the end of the long beach and walks towards her house. The sea is very far out again and he walks along the sand, enshrouded by the mist, unable to see anything more than a short distance away.

At her house he rings the doorbell and she comes down and lets him in. She seems to have changed in a very short time. She looks unhappy and older. They go up to the attic.

"This isn't four weeks," she says.

They are reserved and quiet in each other's company. No sound enters the room from outside.

"How is it?" he asks.

"It's bad without you. Maybe we should talk about things."

"Do you sleep badly?" he asks.

"No, sleeping is easy. I get so drunk. It's being awake that I'm not so happy with."

"Did you sleep well last night?"

She nods.

"Where?"

She points to the bed.

"All night?"

"This is why it was going wrong. Because of your questions."

"You just said you wanted to talk."

She says nothing.

"I shouldn't have done it but I was here, in this room, early this morning," he says. "I was, you weren't."

"No, it's true I wasn't here. Greg and Louise took me back to their place. They were worried about me."

"So you lied. You didn't sleep here at all, did you?"

She would normally be so angry. Now she just sits down and begins to cry.

"I lied. I didn't sleep here. I was too drunk. They took me home."

She looks up at him with tired, tearful eyes. She seems small, delicate and vulnerable there and he feels a great tenderness towards her. He takes her hands and pulls her to her feet and into his arms.

"I still love you," he says. They hold onto each other. Then he pushes away the top of her T-shirt and kisses her shoulder, pushes back her hair and kisses her neck and earlobe. Their bodies are very much ready for lovemaking but they are held back by their thoughts. She has just lied to him once; should he believe what she says now? She seems weary with sadness, a long way from the exuberantly passionate woman with whom he used to make love. So they lie down together on the bed for a long time. Holding each other but not moving, tender but uncertain. The room is very quiet. She begins to fall asleep but stirs herself.

"How's the work?" he says.

"Oh, I've been working a lot. I've done a great deal in the last two weeks." Her smile barely covers her sadness. Her attempt at cheeriness is pitiful.

"Can I see?"

He raises himself into a sitting position at the end of the bed while she rummages among her canvasses. She raises four of them, one after another, for him to see. This is the point at which their relationship ends. She is standing at the foot of the bed holding up old paintings, attempting a weak smile, lines of tiredness and unhappiness around her eyes. He is sitting on the bed looking confused and sad and seems unable to speak. He gets up and looks at the paintings carefully. Her work mattered to him more than he ever succeeded in expressing. He knows each of these paintings well enough, they were all painted some time ago. He can ask her more questions and try to understand. But which answers will be lies and which will be truth? How long ago did the lies begin? He doesn't know what to say.

"These are old paintings."

She looks away from him and takes a deep breath before answering.

"Yes."

He walks out of the door, down the stairs and out into the thick mist coming in off the sea.

He walks along the beach, hidden from the rest of the world, unable to see anything but his immediate surroundings: wet sand, white air. He is in a state of shock. He tries to think of what he will do in the next few days, weeks, months. He makes a mental list of activities, things he has to do with his work, things he enjoys alone, friends he will spend time with. None of this matters or has any meaning for him. Nothing will compare to their life together. The fulfilment. The happiness.

He's stunned. He makes his way down to the water's edge. Nothing seems real enough to make him feel truly alive. It has been very mild weather and he knows that the sea is still warm from earlier in the year. Perhaps it will bring him alive, will shake him out of this sense of non-existence. He takes off all his clothes and wades out into the motionless shallow water. Even before it's deep enough to swim he can't see the beach through the mist. When it's deeper he drops down into the water and swims a few strokes. He duck-dives and swims along the bottom with his eyes open, seeing about as much as he could see above the water. Then he stands waist-deep, watching the water run down his cold body. His body was special to him because it was special to her. No one else had known him in such tender detail or wanted him so much. It feels terribly unlikely that anyone will ever care for him, or be cared for by him, in the same way again. He is getting cold, turns and swims towards the shore. After a while he stops to touch the bottom with his feet. It doesn't seem to be getting any shallower. He swims again hoping that the cold emptiness of the sea will clear his mind of the thoughts that are crowding in. But in the sensory deprivation of cold salt-water and white mist he sees only images of her. He swims faster as if the effort will save him from these thoughts.

When he tires he puts his feet down to rest, he should be in very shallow water by now. He can't touch the bottom. He turns and swims in a panic back in the direction, he thinks, from which he came. Then he stops and, still unable to touch the bottom, treads water, turning very slowly, listening and looking for anything to give him a sense of his position. He can't see or hear anything of the land. He realises that he could now quite easily swim out to sea and drown. He's very frightened and he doesn't want to die. He has to decide on a direction, swim, and hope. He swims again, stopping to reach down with his feet from time to time, his fear growing.

Eventually he touches the bottom and soon he is wading ashore. The sand feels very good against the soles of his feet. Of course he can't see his clothes and must run up and down naked, close to the sea's edge, until he finds them. Then he dresses, shivering, knowing he will soon be in a warm car and then later in front of a hot fire at home. Just for a moment it feels good to be alive. He smiles.

THIRTEEN

We carry the full sacks of carrots to the bottom of the field, there isn't space to take the tractor up between the rows of vegetables. Each time we put the heavy sacks down we rest for a moment before going back up for more. Here under the trees there's a strong sense of the changing season. There's a new smell that hasn't been in the air for a long time, damp soil and rotting vegetation, fertile decay. The long grass here lies in rank clumps. Scattered over the surface are the first of this year's fallen leaves, yellow and red from a wild cherry, green and yellow from an ash. In the hedgerow, individual trees stand out, changing colour and losing leaves ahead of their green neighbours. This morning the air was clear and cool. There's a clarity of light that comes with this time of year, and a vibrant range of colours replaces the uniform green of the past months. The changes are gradual, predictable and comforting. The certainty of season.

At lunchtime we take a trailer-load of carrots down to the farmyard and then sit in the sunshine to eat. It is sheltered here and warm enough at this time of day to take our shirts off, perhaps for the last time this year. When we have finished eating Julian goes indoors for a moment, returns with the pages I gave him this morning and begins to read. I lean back against the wall of the farmhouse and close my eyes to enjoy the feeling of the sun's heat on my skin. I have a different feeling about him reading my story now. These are the words that I wrote last night, they are still fresh in my mind, and he reads them sitting right here beside me. Something of the distance between writing and reading, between writer and reader, has diminished. I keep my eyes shut and try to enjoy the sun while he reads. Actually I'm with him in those pages. When I can tell from the sound of his movements that he has finished, I open my eyes.

He is quiet for a moment, reflecting on what he has read. I can't tell from his expression what he is thinking.

"It's a bit sudden isn't it?" he says. "The ending of it all."

"Maybe."

"Was it hard to write that?"

"Yes."

I look across the yard at Julian's sailing boat sticking out of the end of the barn. I have to squint against the sunlight. Neither of us have anything to say for a while.

"Well I'm relieved it's over but you must feel strange with it all finished – no more writing to do. Will you write something else?"

"No, I'm not a writer, I'm just dabbling. You know my painting and my photography are much more important to me. I've got two exhibitions coming up soon."

"Why did you write it?"

"I don't know. Something to do with working with you. To do with having a connection, through you, with someone from the past."

"I feel a bit used."

"No, that's not fair. You've been encouraging me. You didn't have to employ me and you didn't have to read anything. Surely you had your reasons."

I have my eyes shut again. It's a good way to hold a conversation, just the sound of your own and someone else's voices. I can't see the expression on Julian's face so I have a certain freedom to say what I want. The confessional must be like this – two anonymous voices, no eye-contact. But now, as ever, we will both hold back as much as we say. I hope.

"All these months of working together and you still won't ask me about her," Julian says. "There's a real person we don't talk about."

"I think that's best for me."

"You're a selfish man, John. Do you know that?"

"What have I done?"

"I think you used her. You learnt a great deal from her art and now you're doing okay."

"You don't know. People learn from each other all the time. Is this a jealousy thing? Because she and I are both artists?"

"And then you think it's okay to write about her."

"I don't think you like me very much," I say.

"I do actually. Just not at this moment."

The sun goes behind a cloud and I can feel a cool breeze on my skin. I have to open my eyes and put my T-shirt on.

"Why does the wind pick up when the sun goes behind a cloud?" I ask. "I don't understand."

"The wind doesn't pick up, it's just that you can't feel it when the heat of the sun is on your skin. It's a changed perception." He looks at me and grins. "That's the sort of thing you're interested in, isn't it?"

We spend the rest of the day up on the field pulling carrots. It gets steadily cooler during the afternoon. As the sun declines the quality of the light changes, it is startlingly clear and the colours are warm and strong.

"You know the growing season is more or less over," Julian says. "And there's no planting-out, the weeds stop growing soon. I can do most of the late harvesting myself."

"So there won't be much more work for me then?"

"That's what I'm coming to."

"You're the boss Julian. But there is one thing."

"Yes?"

"One more chapter."

"But I thought it was all over."

It is the middle of the night, he has been on the sea for fourteen hours without a rest, he is exhausted and his state of mind is chaotic. It is dark and there is a storm. Now he turns the boat away from the land and faces out to sea. It is all he can do. He has been foolish but tomorrow it will be alright, he will finish his journey and leave the boat, the sea, his pointless memories. Tonight he is obliged to heave-to, to set the boat pointing into the wind and waves with his reefed-in mainsail to one side and his jib to the other, turning into the storm like a weather-vane in order to ride it out. Tomorrow the wind will have dropped, the sea calmed, and he will be able to go home. He has struggled half a day and part of the night along this section of the coast, sometimes scared, sometimes exhilarated and happy. Excitement and fear have given him the energy and concentration to carry on, but finally he has had to set the boat up in this way, safely pointing into the waves and away from the lee shore.

He remembers his awkward indecision in the morning. Waiting for the tide to lift him off the muddy harbour bottom, wanting to not believe the forecast of a force six wind. An irritating middle-aged yachtie looking down from the quayside and muttering vague truisms on the difficulties of sailing single-handed, saying 'but you look as if you know what you're doing' while casting an eye on the warps that had snagged in the night and left the boat at an angle as the tide dropped. Listening to the rain fall, looking over the chart of the bay and the nautical almanac, working out estimates of speed and time of arrival at various harbours down the coast. Finally, impatient to be home, setting off at midday in a lull in the weather. Hoping that no one would see him and note his foolishness.

And then an extraordinary afternoon of fine sailing, of handling the boat better than he has before, a beam-reach taking him quickly down the coast. Then the storm coming on. Tacking to get away from the shore and the boat juddering against badly hit waves. Fear. Large waves breaking in white crests all around him. The sea writhing under an incessant wind. The waves getting larger and steeper, the troughs between them deeper. Sometimes the sea falling away from underneath him and the boat tipping into space, the bow burying itself in the water and the next wave coming over the deck and over him before lifting him up again. Great swings of the mast from side to side as the boat rolls. Noise, wind, rain. A realisation that he cannot make harbour in these conditions. Night coming on and the sea repeatedly coming over the deck.

Now he has heaved to and knows that it will be alright. This is a safe way to spend the night on the water. He must only stay awake and watch the sails, tolerate the cold, the wet and his tiredness and wait for dawn. He had dreamt of finding some sort of peace out here, a meditative state, an empty mind. Instead he has been obsessively looking back at the land and thinking about two people on the shore.

They walk along the promenade towards the harbour, stopping to look at the sea, stopping to look at each other, outside of time. How long have they stood here, while others have come and gone? Perhaps the tide has turned. 'What are they doing?' some passer-by asks himself, 'they were there an hour ago, what can they be saying to each other?' Only how it is for them now, how it was yesterday when he came to her unexpectedly, how it was the day before when they forgot to get off the bus and walked a mile back. And what she thought when he said... And what he thought when she said... And how it felt when they made love in the middle of the night and again at dawn. And then silent while he looks at the particular way her hair lies on her forehead and she thinks he looks beautiful all dressed in blue.

She mustn't laugh, her ribs still hurt from the car accident. But there's a man on the jetty striking such a preposterous stance as he looks out to sea, one hand ostentatiously raised to shield his eyes from the sun, one hand clutching a shooting stick. And the way he walks now as if all the world watches him. He smiles and makes her look towards the man again – his shooting stick has caught between the timbers of the jetty and he stumbles, losing all his dignity for a moment. So she splutters out laughter and he holds her against him to steady her injured body. He holds her as still as he can but her eyes fill with tears of laughter and then of pain as she winces and cries out. They stand motionless against each other until the pain subsides.

The storm continues. His fear is increased when from time to time the clouds part and a gibbous moon lights up the sea to show him the size of the waves. The moon comes out again now after being hidden for maybe two hours. It has dropped towards the horizon but not moved across the sky. But some time has passed, it can't be exactly on the port beam as it was before. But it is. Time is playing a spiteful trick on him. He has day-dreamed – *night*-dreamed – for hours, and the moon has not moved around the sky. He has had nothing to do but watch the waves; the boat will always turn into the wind and ride out the storm. Yes, that's it, the boat has slowly turned with the changing wind and now points further round to the west, keeping the moon in the same position. He looks over his shoulder but he's too far out to see any lights on the distant land. Perhaps the wind is dropping now. Of course the waves will go on for a while but some time in the morning he will be able to take a compass-bearing and turn back towards the shore. He would like to be less cold. He would like to be less hungry and tired. He would like different thoughts.

It has been a good day together, just walking along the prom towards the harbour. She stops to buy cigarettes and he thinks of one way that she could save money and pay him back what she owes. The light across the bay is hazy in the heat and they can't see beyond the nearest headlands.

"Can you look for a part-time job again sometime? There's no hurry but I need that money back eventually."

"I just know that I will sell something in the new gallery. I've really got to tidy up and frame a few things before it opens. Be patient with me, will you? I really do have to get on with my work at the moment."

The light is cold and hard on the horizon and on the jutting land around the bay. They walk faster and will reach the harbour before sunset.

"Perhaps you can cut down on how much you spend. But it doesn't matter – it's okay, forget about it for a while."

"You like this don't you? A nice little long-term grudge against me that you can wheel out whenever you're in a bad mood. Don't worry – I pay my debts."

He should have brought the subject up later. This early in the morning she was bound to be irritable if he mentioned it. The sky darkens and a fine drizzle obscures sight of land and sea. They hurry on towards the harbour, side by side like a grumpy old couple who have done this for too long.

The sky seems lighter, the clouds are clearing, the wind has dropped, perhaps the waves are less now. The boat is certainly steadier. Soon it will be dawn and he can turn and head towards the harbour. Now he will go down below and rummage for food. He feels sick but he must try to get something inside him for the last leg. He will clip himself into the harness again when he comes up; he could fall asleep at any time. His mind wanders, leaving images of the past and moving on to visions of the future.

So many years have passed since they have seen each other or spoken or written. Walking together here again, along the prom towards the harbour, is like a dream. And she has mellowed over the years. They are able to talk of the past with honesty and without anger. Their feelings are strong but this time there is a chance of working out the problems. Perhaps later in the day they will make love somewhere. She looks well, a very little grey in her hair, more at peace with the world. She has put on weight which is good – she must be looking after herself. She turns as if to kiss him. Just these feelings now. Later today explanations and under-standing, catching up on news, shared memories. Time has allowed him to forgive her everything. To trust her again.

So many years since they have seen each other but now her car is parked by the harbour again. He wonders where she is and hopes they don't meet. He feels only anger, such anger. Hatred in proportion to the love he once felt. He turns and walks hurriedly away, not trusting his words if by chance they should meet and find themselves obliged to speak to one another. He would say such ugly hateful things. He doesn't see her, but as he walks along he says the words under his breath.

So many years later he has found himself walking towards the harbour again. What if he should meet her here? A frightening thought but it makes him smile. He knows that his mind is playing tricks on him, but the person coming towards him certainly looks like her. More than looks like. He is holding his breath. He isn't dreaming. He knows that he is smiling broadly. As soon as she notices him she crosses, quite deliberately, to the other side of the road. She lets him know that she has seen him but avoids looking in his direction. She doesn't speak. Her face holds no expression.

The sky is clear and bright, the wind has dropped to a breeze, the moon has set and soon the sun will rise up above the low hills along the coast. He has turned the boat and recognises familiar landmarks on the shore. He sails on towards the harbour.

As the morning brightens the wind decreases. He is frustrated at his slow progress. Closer to the land now he should get a clear impression of his movement along the coast towards the end point of his journey. But he is moving slowly. He works hard at adjusting the sails to make the best of the small breeze but he is exhausted and his concentration is poor. Perhaps it doesn't matter – if the wind fades to nothing, he can use the inboard diesel engine to drive him along. The boat will roll badly in the waves that still have much of the force of the storm in them, but at least he will get home. He goes below and looks at the almanac to check that the tide won't have gone too far out by the time he reaches the harbour. There are two-and-a-half hours either side of low water during which he won't be able to get in – but surely he will be there before then.

Painfully tired now he works out his exact position by taking sightings of landmarks and drawing two converging lines on the chart. He has a device that tells him his speed through the water. With this information he can work out how long it will take him to get there. He looks at the almanac and tide-tables again. The sails are dropping from lack of wind and he isn't going to make it before low water. After a storm like that it is hard to imagine that he could be stuck out here for lack of wind. But it's true. He is almost in tears with exhaustion and the frustration of not being able to get home. He cannot spend another day on the water.

He is close to a wide estuary that has a small town with something like a harbour at its entrance. He starts the boat's engine, takes all sail down and heads in. He looks again at the chart and almanac. There is a sand bar to negotiate and two buoys mark the channel. The large waves are helping him in and he makes very good progress. He can see the buoys coming up fast and will soon have to turn to avoid the bar. The tide is going out and a massive volume of water is leaving the estuary and meeting the incoming waves. In the shallow water the waves are forced up into large peaks with deep troughs between them. The boat begins to see-saw and crash awkwardly against these waves, each impact shaking him. In windless fine weather he has managed to put himself in the middle of some of the most difficult water in the whole bay. And he will have to turn broadside to these waves to avoid running aground.

He is now close to the sand-bar. He turns hard to starboard and is immediately swamped by a large breaking wave that crashes onto the deck and nearly knocks him over. He is angry.

He starts to swear at the sea, the worst words he can think of shouted at the top of his voice. The waves retaliate, some of them swamping the boat, washing in through the cabin door that he has left open, some of them leaning the boat precariously on its side. Without sail the boat is unstable and rolling wildly. He has had three distress flares in his pocket all night but has been determined not to use them. Now he lets go of the wheel and fires two of them into the sky in quick succession. The orange smoke drifts down through the still morning air as the boat capsizes.

FOURTEEN

The sea is a great expanse of grey-green and blue cold water, stretching under an opaque winter sky. Across its surface runs a swell, large rollers generated by the wind of a few days ago, continuing their motion from the west until they come up against the land. There the line of waves changes, refracting around headlands and bending to take on something of the shape of the shoreline. The waves, as they approach the shore, are large and smoothly-rounded, like whale-backs. Here they are meeting a shingle beach, each wave hitting with some force, then dissipating among the stones with a rattle and a sigh. The sound is rhythmic and might be soothing. The air is still but the waves have travelled from far away, where there was once a wind, and now, with the momentum of past events, they move steadily onto the shore.

Above the beach, at the foot of a small valley that runs down to the sea, is a large, mostly empty building, the old stable block for the grand house that once stood close by. It is now used mainly for the storage of farm implements but also has a flat upstairs above the stables. The building faces south, looking over the stream to the other side of the valley. Only a small window in its gable-end looks out towards the sea. There are no other houses around and it is a bleak lonely place, cold and exposed, with none of the softening influence of the trees that grow further inland.

A man stands at the top of the steps that lead up to the flat and rings the doorbell repeatedly. He takes off one glove and knocks on the wooden door. There is no answer. He walks down the steps and along a short path of frozen mud to the beach, his shoulders hunched against the cold. It has been freezing for days, with the temperatures falling further each night under clear skies. Now there is cloud cover and something like rain, so there should be a thaw.

But where water has been dripping from the cliffs there are still icicles and there is ice on the rocks where the stream flows onto the beach. Julian walks down the beach and looks, from a safe distance, at the cold waves. Then he goes back and up onto the cliff path from which he can look at the view across the bay. Half an hour later he returns to the flat and knocks again. She lets him in.

"Thank you for coming today," she says. "Did you knock earlier? I was under the covers and had a feeling that someone was around but when I got up I couldn't see you."

"I wish you would look after yourself. It's freezing in here." Julian goes straight to the stove, opens it and begins to clean it out with a brush and shovel. He looks up at her, "Please, please keep warm. At least do that."

He goes out and down the steps, returning after a while with a heap of kindling and logs. She has found some old newspaper and crumpled it into the grate. She kneels close to the stove as Julian arranges the kindling and puts a match to the fire. Then he does the washing-up. She pulls a chair in close to the stove and watches passively.

"I'm so sorry Jules but I'm not saying anything am I? I think I'm losing the power of speech living here. And you're being so practical and kind."

He turns from his chores, "You know I'm more worried about you than I've ever been. That's really saying something. You need to hear this. Do you understand what I'm saying?"

She nods.

"Eat and keep warm – at least those two things. Have you eaten anything today?"

"Cornflakes."

He puts more wood on the fire then digs out some potatoes, carrots and onions from the back of the cupboard. He sets about making a huge vegetable-stew that would feed a family.

"What are you doing? You're insane making so much."

"This is for other days too. All you have to do is heat it up."

The room is getting a little warmer but their breath still forms clouds of steam in front of them as they speak. Julian goes and brings in more kindling and logs and stacks them near the stove. He stirs the stew. Then, at last, he takes his coat off, walks across to her and wraps his arms around her in a warm hug.

"Be crazy. Be the mad artist who lives by the sea, drinks too much, talks to herself and paints day and night. Forget how to talk to people and what day of the week it is."

He holds her at arm's length and looks at her with concern.

"But look after yourself too. Eat. Heat the place – there are plenty of logs downstairs."

She looks sad. "Sorry," she says. "And thank you."

They eat their stew sitting on hard chairs either side of the stove. Then Julian asks her to show him her work. There are two big new canvasses to look at since last week, both unfinished gaudy abstract works that might be something to do with landscape. His eyes move quickly from one to the other.

"Wonderful," he says. "I'm glad you're working."

The room is warmer now but he continues to add wood to the fire until there is no more space.

"You think it's like the soup," she says. "If you get the room really hot it will last for a few days. Julian you're so kind to me and you let me be as mad as I want. I don't deserve it."

She kisses him on the cheek and stands with her arms around him and her head on his shoulder. He strokes her hair with his finger tips until she moves away.

She makes coffee for the two of them while he watches.

"You never used computers, did you?" he asks.

"Me, what for?"

"I mean to do things with pictures, you know, with photographs."

"I did a little bit, a long time ago. But it's boy's stuff. Crap really. Why do you ask?"

"It's nothing. I was talking to someone who thinks that stuff is important."

"Okay." She looks at him curiously. She gives him his coffee, sits opposite, and lights a cigarette. He looks at her new paintings. "You've been working hard."

"So you've been talking to someone who's been doing art and computers, have you?"

"Yes."

"Is it who I think it might be?"

"Yes."

"I wish you wouldn't."

"Why not?"

"I just wish you wouldn't, that's all. Have you been talking about me behind my back?"

"No. Anyway he's miles away now and I haven't seen him since the end of the growing season."

She looks both sad and angry. She looks as if she would like to cover her ears with her hands and not hear his words. They sit in silence for a while.

"You know Gareth and Olivia are worried about you too. He wonders if he can come over some time and talk to you about things."

"I like Gareth, you can send him over. But talk about what? Anyway I don't always answer the door."

She gets up and starts to tidy the room in a half-hearted way. She looks across at Julian.

"You haven't seen him since the end of the growing season?"

"That's right."

"You gave him a job, didn't you? Without telling me."

"Yes I did."

"All summer?"

"Yes. I didn't want to tell you if it was going to be a problem."

"You spent all that time together?"

She is angry now and her tidying becomes a random movement of things from place to place.

"You can't do that to me," she says. "You have no right to do that."

"I'm sorry but I have every right. I employ the people I

choose. I just decided not to tell you. And I can do that too."

Her eyes are narrow with anger, her body very tense. Julian finds that her mood is affecting him.

"He doesn't talk about you. He doesn't ask. He doesn't want to know anymore."

"Without telling me, Julian. That's the worst thing. All summer and not saying a word to me."

"Why are you so upset when I employ your former lover?" he asks.

It hurts him that this man from her past has such a strong effect on her. He starts to pace up and down the room between the clutter of her artist's materials. Then he stops and looks out of the window at the sea, trying to regain calm, to avoid crisis. But he doesn't feel that he should always have to be the one who is thoughtful and considerate.

"You know he hates you now."

Her anger has been building. For a moment she is rigid with self-control. She pushes her hair back away from her face. He turns and looks away as she moves towards him. Then there's a sudden movement and he feels her fist very hard against his cheek, close to his left eye. A bone-against-bone pain.

He moves around her very fast and very carefully. He picks up a half-empty coffee cup and throws it with extraordinary force against the opposite wall, where it shatters, a stain of coffee up to the ceiling and shards flung to each corner of the room. He stands facing the wall, not looking towards her, his hands shaking. She looks at him with round eyes, shocked, bewildered. It happened very fast. He diverted his anger around her with care and grace as if protecting her from some external harm. She is reminded of protective tendernesses of the past. For a moment there is silence then she takes his hands and rests herself lightly, cautiously against him.

Soon they are on the floor, some clothes discarded, moving hard against each other. They reach a state where, for both of them, the only conscious sense is that of physical pleasure. No thoughts. No self-awareness. No knowledge of the involuntary sounds they make. Only later do they regain some sort of consciousness and find themselves in the corner of the room, sweating, tear-stained, bruised. Breathing hard amid a chaos of fallen books, photographs and the shards of a coffee cup.

They have disentangled themselves from each other. She has straightened her clothes and is sitting by the stove. She lights a cigarette and tries to stop herself from crying. She doesn't succeed.

"It's never been like that before," Julian says. "We've never fought, we've always talked it through."

There's a long silence. Just the muffled sound of the sea beyond the window and the noise of wood settling in the stove. She gradually becomes calmer.

"You still love him, don't you?" he says.

She nods her head in agreement.

"And I hate him too. Just as much. You know when I hit you, I'm so sorry I did that. It wasn't you. It was him that I wanted to hurt."

He tries to understand this. He turns it over in his mind for a while.

"I'm sorry," she says again.

"What about after that? What we did next. Was that me or was that him too? Because that wasn't the same either."

"How calm you are, Jules. I can talk to you because you're so kind and sane. I could never, never talk to John like that. And I could never speak honestly to him. There was too much emotion."

"You haven't answered my question."

She takes a deep breath.

"I started making love to you. You were so careful with your anger. Careful not to hurt me. But I guess it wasn't only you. I was with someone else for a while. Someone from the past." She smiles, "You see how faithless I am. I change partner halfway through making love."

Like a small child she is crying and laughing at the same time.

"Maybe John was right about me all the time."

FIFTEEN

Julian isn't in so I walk across the fields to Gareth and Olivia's house. I have been away in the city all winter, in another world, other company and a different state of mind. It was the right thing to do. Now I'm in the countryside again and I can open my senses. I can look around without seeing ugliness, use my ears without being assailed by harsh noise, and I can smell air that isn't full of fumes. There are bright flowers in the hedgerow-bottom and the birds are singing. I can't explain the pleasure of these things to my city friends without seeming foolish. It would be nice to be able to enjoy all this, but being here again brings up some uncomfortable feelings.

Gareth and Olivia's door is wide open and the dogs are wagging their tails so I walk right in. Julian is there too. They are in the middle of a deep conversation which they immediately drop, leaving a silence. I feel awkward.

"But John, we're so surprised to see you," Olivia says. "I'm sorry, you left us speechless for a moment. You look different. How are you?"

They are very welcoming of course but there's an awkwardness that I don't know how to interpret. I suppose I just interrupted something that they can't continue in front of me. They give me tea and biscuits and we make polite conversation. I hear myself using a strange rural vocabulary of season, weather and the land. Words that I couldn't use in the city. Then Julian walks back with me to his place, where I have left my car.

"So you didn't miss country life at all?" he asks.

"The countryside in winter? Rainy, dark at four o'clock in the afternoon and nowhere to go. No, I didn't miss that."

"I think it was strange for you spending the summer with me.

I bet you were relieved in a way to be gone. Am I right?"

"You're right," I say.

"And writing. Have you given up that?"

"Oh that. Yes I've had better things to do with my time."

"And you haven't missed it?"

"Well I did as it happens, it's a different sort of creativity from my other stuff. But it was good to stop – it seemed so self-indulgent for one thing. I only realised afterwards that it was quite fulfilling. It mattered to me more than I knew. It seemed meaningful and worthwhile. I know that sounds stupid."

As we walk up the track to Julian's place I'm reminded of the strange mixture of closeness and distance in our relationship.

"So it wasn't worthwhile?" he asks.

"Well I'm not a writer. Any real meaning in doing it seems illusory to me now. Words are only words, aren't they? Very temporary things. I mean, I didn't intend anyone to read it."

"But I read it."

"Yes, I know."

Julian opens the gate and we walk into the farmyard. He points to the empty barn. "I sold it to someone who had enough time to fix it up and get it on the water."

Everything changes, things come to an end. Still, I'm very surprised to see Julian's barn with no boat in it. And it's strange that I was in the farmyard earlier in the day and I didn't notice that it had gone. The boat was the beginning of my story. I would never have started writing in the first place if it hadn't been for that half-restored boat in the barn.

"I never had time to work on it," Julian continues. "Maybe a little bit in winter, but then it's too cold to do much of that sort of thing. It made a lot of sense to get the barn usable again and admit to myself that I would never finish the thing and get it on the water."

"Well I feel sad that you sold it," I say. "It's good to have a dream standing by. It wouldn't matter much whether it got used or not."

"I know. Logic and reason got the better of me for a moment

and I accepted a good offer. I do regret selling it. Not because it was any use to me – it just sat there – but now I feel that I've become all work and no play."

We're standing looking at the empty space where the boat was. I find myself remembering the time I hid in it because a certain person's car was parked in the farmyard. That was daft. It seems unlikely now. Did that really happen or did I dream it? I hope Julian doesn't bring the subject up.

"Talking of work," he says, "if you're staying around, for old time's sake and to help me out..."

"Yes?"

"Do you want a day's work tomorrow? Something quite pleasant. Weather forecast is for sunshine all day. I can lend you some old clothes if you want."

In the morning Julian and Olivia are in the farmyard when I arrive. The sun is very bright and it's warming up already. Julian is in high spirits.

"Perfect soil conditions for planting out. Olivia's helping me too. She's quit soliciting." He grins.

"I'm still a solicitor," she corrects him and turns to me. "I've gone back to part-time again, that's all. And I work some days for Julian. He pays about a tenth of what I normally get but really I should be paying him for the therapeutic value of being out on the land. I really enjoy it."

Julian has the work already set up for us and has a cabbage planter fitted to the back of the tractor. The machine cuts furrows through the soil, drops the plants into it and firms the soil around them. Two people – today it's me and Olivia – sit on the back and place the small plants in special grippers as it goes along. Julian bought the machine with some of the money he got from selling the boat. He drives the tractor and we sit behind putting the plants in place. He stops often to check the depth of planting or change some cogs so that the plants are spaced out more evenly. Julian's little tractor is fairly quiet, the sun is warm, our actions are rhythmic. As we get used to the work we are able to relax and talk as we go along. The machine is at least thirty years old and has instructions in French written on it. So Olivia and I feel we are in some dreamy pastoral French film. We imagine that Julian will offer us red wine with our lunch. We attempt to speak French to each other. It's a shame that Julian is separated from us by the noise of the tractor and his need to concentrate on driving in a straight line. When we stop for a tea-break he walks up and down the field checking that the plants are well in place. He pushes his fingers into the soft soil to make sure that only the surface is drying in the sunshine. When he sits with us to drink his tea our conversation pauses. There's some sort of understanding between him and Olivia, something serious that brings them together.

"Is Gareth well?" I ask her.

"He's very well – just working too hard, but that will never change."

"You don't ever get involved with the farm-work at your place then?"

"No, that's exactly right. I don't get involved. You see, working for Julian, he's the boss and I'm in the carefree situation of just doing what I'm told. But with Gareth I would be trying to change things and we would row. Husband-and-wife teams working together aren't always a good idea. We're happier to see each other at the end of the day when we work separately."

It does turn out to be sunny all day. At lunch time I take my shirt off (Julian's shirt actually) and stretch out on the grass at the bottom of the field. The sun feels very good on my skin. The first butterflies of the year are drifting around on gentle breezes, there are good green smells in the air and a bird sings on a branch above me. Winter in the city is a distant dream. Olivia is talking to Julian and still dropping French phrases in when she can. I feel as if I'm on holiday abroad. This is nice.

Towards the end of the day, Julian asks Olivia to change places with him and drive the tractor for a while. He sits beside me and when he feels confident that the plants are going in as he wants we can talk of the differences between city life and country life. Then he's steering the talk back to my story.

"I think you'll take up writing again some day," he says.

"No way. Okay, it feels very fulfilling and meaningful when you're doing it. But then it's over, and it was all about nothing. None of it was real."

"That's what you keep saying. But don't you miss it afterwards?"

"Oh yes. That's the irony. There was no point to it. It didn't mean anything. And it hurts when it's over." I laugh.

Olivia has driven us to the end of a row and we stop putting plants into the machine.

"No," I say, "I won't be doing that again."

We don't talk much for the remainder of the day. Julian is thoughtful. It seems as if he might be angry with me and I wonder what I've said or done. Before I go we are in his kitchen and he thanks me and pays me for the day's work. Then he passes me a cardboard folder stuffed with papers.

"Your turn to do the reading now," he says.

I have the impression of some stifled emotion in him but I can't guess what it's about.

"Someone has asked me to give you these to read. I suppose I must."

I take the folder from him, touched by his seriousness. I can't imagine what it is that he is giving me.

SIXTEEN

Dear Jules

My name is Catrin and I am an alcoholic. This is what I have to say every time at the beginning of group therapy. I'm an alcoholic and I'm in the desert – that's what I call this place. Like a lot of the others here I get pretty thirsty sometimes. Not for water though, you can imagine. They ask me when it started and I say after a relationship many years ago. That's wrong. It's denial they say. Everything is denial here and I'm told it all started much earlier. Whatever. Denial is not a river in Egypt – that's what it says on the poster in the corridor. It made me laugh first time I saw it but now it's wearing thin. Denial is not a river in the desert. OK.

We have to talk about the powerlessness and damage of our addiction. Always always damage. It's always bad, it was never fun, it always hurt people. That's not true and I get into trouble for saying it. Tell us when you were drunk or stoned and it was good for people around you they say. I don't like the fact that they're always right and everything I say that doesn't fit is wrong. So I tell that after that car accident I was on a lot of painkillers and they were some sort of opiate and really really nice (and I pretended I'd lost my prescription and got more). I tell them about a room by the beach and an old boyfriend looking after me and it was like the only time he wasn't selfish and really took care of me (not like you Jules you always take care of me) and I was so stoned that I never got angry with him for being around. And it was great. I was stoned all day and everything was still and calm and the only noise was the sea sound coming through the window at night.

This is in group therapy. Everybody's listening and I just jabber on like a crazy woman who hasn't spoken to anyone for years (a bit true). I get really into it. Looking at the moon through the window at night. Hot. No clothes on. And I'm there for a moment and there's silence in the room. About that relationship, the counsellor says. It sounds very loving. Being stoned sounds nice. That relationship ended didn't it? he says. Yes. And were you drinking, what happened to make it go wrong? He sounds like a loving man and you were very special to each other, he says. Yes. What happened? He was selfish and jealous and possessive and stuff I say. So it ended. I'm spitting out words, angry now they tell me (every five minutes they tell me I'm angry so of course pretty soon I am). It didn't go wrong because of drink then? the counsellor says and I say no it was afterwards. It was because of him. It was because of him that you started drinking badly? His fault yes, yes, yes. And they're all sitting round looking like they know it all and they start saying blame, blame, blame and of course denial and so on. So what was his name, the man who cared for you after the accident in that room you described with the noise of the sea coming through the window and so forth? Who was he? They press your buttons, they know how to do it and they do it on purpose. What was his name and I say John. There's a big box of kleenex in every room here. They get through more than anywhere else in the world. I say his name was John and I'm crying and I really didn't expect this to happen.

There's a big board with all our names on it and stuff written up there every week that we have to say and do. So it's Tuesday morning and someone writes up the board. Catrin: share three examples of powerlessness (this is not being able to stop) and damage to (wait for it) John. Written up there for everyone to see. But that was years ago I say. And he had a good time not like people around me later when I seriously started drinking (not like you Jules, I'm sorry – one week in this place and yes I can see a little what I've done to people). So this is what I start with. Digging this stuff up. I tell them about not answering the door and the cold and icicles on the beach and how you forced the door because you thought I was dead and then you had to do a lot of carpentry. I'm not thinking hard but this sounds like damage to me and so I've done what they ask. Now it seems that the first couple of days I was in here (a week ago and I can't remember it – weird) I talked and talked about my place by the beach where I was painting so much and you used to come and visit and how cold it was and I got ill and you and Gareth persuaded me to come here etc. So they know about all that and about you breaking the door down to see if I was dead. So it wasn't John they say – you're telling us about someone else. I thought I'd given them what they wanted but I'm always in trouble here. They say I lie. They say I need to get a hold of reality. Fuck reality I say and I'm halfway up the drive (posh house, long drive) and there's this seedy old guy (nice man as it turns out) who's asking me what I will do now I'm leaving? Have a drink of course. I need one and I deserve one after all that crap. And everything will be alright then? he says, and guess what I'm crying again and walking back down the drive to the posh house (more of which later).

So denial is not a river in the desert. This is the desert. Powerlessness. Damage to someone from so far back but I really have to do what they say now or I'm out. And I need to share all my thoughts and feelings with my 'group' and not write to you. Well I promised to write and so I do. The post-tray is by the door of the general office and it's easy to drop a letter in when no one is looking so I will write again soon. Dearest Jules thank you. This place might be the right thing for me (I don't know) and you've made it happen. And thank you to Gareth for helping with the money for me to be here. Give him a kiss for me. I will write again soon. My name is Catrin and I am an alcoholic...

All my love...

~

Dearest Jules

I'm in trouble again. I'm on a cliff edge I'm told. I did the same thing again – told a story about something I did to you when I was meant to be talking about someone else. They make me feel like a real shit. Double shit right now and I have to tell you why. The story I told is about a time I stole money from your wallet. I'm sorry, I meant to put it back later and I didn't. I told them I was borrowing it and I meant to return it. I got the D word again of course and they're right. What did I steal it for? A bottle. I put all these things to the back of my mind. These people here force them to the front and I feel like a real shit. You stole, they say, from your best friend/lover (whatever) to buy a bottle of vodka. Yes I did. Sorry. They make you feel shameful here. They don't pull their punches. But it was so long ago I can't remember. And it was before I was so bad. Of course they reach for the D word. Why, they say, do you avoid looking at that particular relationship? Another D word so maybe it's triple shit, this time it's defiance. Defiance is not doing every single thing I'm asked. I'm not defiant I would just like to be treated with a little more respect.

I'm angry and I have a clever stupid way of getting at them. I tell everybody about the time I hit you but I tell it like it was John. So I'm deliberately seeming to comply and cleverly stupidly doing something else. This is weird. I hate the counsellors they're always right. Denial, yes. Defiance, yes, I guess so. Lies, yes all the time, I'm doing it all the time like it's been so much my way over the years. Angry, yes. Did I say only triple shit. Quadruple, quintuple, whatever. Oh Julian I'm crying again. Tears on the page as I write like some deeply crap novel. I didn't think it would hurt this much. You can't imagine.

My name is Catrin and I am an alcoholic. Today I will share three examples of damage to John. My damaging John!! That man walked out of my life one day without a single word of explanation. I picked up a picture and I was mixed up and said I'd painted it that week and it was an old one and he walked out on me and never contacted me again. He thought I was screwing someone else. He was so jealous all the time. I wasn't seeing anyone else because there couldn't be anyone else. Not then. He left me like I was nothing at all and I started drinking. They want me to tell of damage to John. It's on my board again for another week because I didn't do it properly before.

Another rant I'm sorry. Do I say that word too often? How are you? I'm writing like I promised. It's such a hard winter here. I can't imagine you working outdoors in this weather. I hope you are alright. Tell Gareth I'm still here.

All my love

Catrin.

Dearest J

Me again. How are you? I'll say more about how it is here.

We all share rooms. I share mine with a sad middle-aged woman who has been an alcoholic for something like thirty years. She's been nearly dead with operations. She's very worn out and looks older than she really is (not like the heroin addicts who seem remarkably well preserved – surely that's not fair?) It's hard to imagine but once (young) she was a high-class prostitute who made a lot of money and spent a lot of money on drink and drugs. She was wild when she was young. I can't think I've ruined my life like her. I've a chance to stop a bit earlier. She's like some dreary housewife sort so it's weird when she tells me the sex stuff. Yes, it is shameful what she's done. I never did anything like that did I? Oh dear. Maybe I did. Just a guy who had a lot of money and who would buy me drinks for a certain consideration. I only slept with him twice. Not what you would call a relationship. It was my lowest point. I haven't told them yet but I will have to sometime.

The stories I hear in this place. It's all confidential so I've already said more than I should and I won't say more. At least I haven't said any names to you. There's two guys here who have been in prison a lot, both heroin addicts. One very rough – lots of violence. When he talks about his childhood he always bursts into tears. People aren't what they seem. Nothing is. Weird here, much talk of reality. Alright stop lying and denial and so forth. But then you have to believe in what they call a 'higher power'. One counsellor really talks about HP (as he calls it) in such a way that it's like superstition. It's like replacing one non-reality with another. It frightens me very much and I'm resistant to all that stuff. But I admire this man. He's made himself into a very special and worthwhile person and he came from so much unhappiness, drink, abuse, violence etc. How did he come from where he was to where he is now? I ask him. HP, he says. Whatever.

Being good and telling everyone about damage to John. A long time ago we were staying on the coast and I wanted to take photographs of these guys who were building a bridge. It was dark and they were by a campfire drinking. I walked (I was moderately pissed and fearless) across this girder to these guys. John must have been so scared for me. I came back hours later and threw up in the sink. I wanted to take photographs you see. That was the big thing for me then – that was my art. So what was in the picture that made you walk across the bridge, what could you see in the firelight? they ask me. You can probably guess. Bottles. And I was angry with John for being moody about it (yes I was angry with him!) He was trying to stop my art-work with his possessive jealousy – that was the official line in those days. Denial is not a river...

About the counsellor who goes on about HP. A funny thing today. I walk into his room and it's been very hot in these buildings (central heating – I'm not used to it) and I'm in a little vest and skirt and he was so straightforward (I'd like men to always be this straightforward I think) he said 'you look like you've come in here to seduce me. You're distracting looking like that (strong Geordie accent I forgot to tell you) go away and put some more clothes on and we'll get on with business'. Well actually a bit patronising. But I like this guy for being so straightforward. I also like him for being distracted.

Soon it will be four weeks without a drink. Everyone says how much I've changed and how crazy I was when I came in. I didn't realise that I'd got so weird. I was talking to myself out loud (really out loud) quite a lot. I suppose you know all this. Also I've put on weight. I was so thin when I came in that they all thought I was anorexic. They asked a lot of questions and I got the D word quite a lot. Well I'm getting rotund now and I'm alright with it. I walked into the staff room today and there's a polaroid on the wall taken of me when I first came in (one of everyone, not just me). Thin. Dark lines under my eyes. I ran off up the drive a total of three times in that first week (I only told you about one). I was very lucky not to get thrown out. But today I was trying to explain to some heroin addict that if he leaves here (it was very close) it will be because he wants to use again and it will fuck up his children's lives. He thanked me afterwards and gave me a hug (hugs are a big thing in here) and suddenly it's like I'm the perceptive one who understands all this stuff and I'm doing really well and I'm a model for others to follow!! He thanked me. Someone thanked me and that's not happened for a long

long time and suddenly I'm not such a shit. I can do stuff for other people and I feel a tiny bit good about being me and I know this place is good for me and I can make it. I'm crying again Julian – can you believe it? Listen Jules if you've ever got any spare money I think kleenex would be a good investment. We get through lorry loads here and I don't think it's going to change.

Here's a thought about John and his jealousy: it was true, I did have a secret lover. But it wasn't a person it was a bottle. So I hid things from him, behaved suspiciously often enough. And yes they're right – I was already an alcoholic in those days. I just hid it so well from everyone (even myself). You see, I'm still learning!

Warmer and more spring-like today and a bird singing (you would know what kind of bird) and I thought of you. It gave me a deep feeling, that sound. The sound reminded me of love (I don't understand what the connection is). OK let's get honest. The sound reminded me of love and then I started thinking about John. Sorry. Should I be this honest? I've always been honest with you in a way that I wasn't with him. Or have I? I know that I've said 'you are the one that I've always been able to tell the truth to'. It's clever. It sounds like I'm saying 'I speak the truth to you'. But it's a subtle little phrase and it means something less than it might. But I'm trying now. Had a whole thing on lies today. Lies disempower the person on the receiving end. Take away the chance for them to make the right decision. Maybe.

I'm doing well here. Tell Gareth. Feeling good today. Hope you are too.

Lots of love

Catrin.

~

Dear J

Slipped this letter in the tray when no one was looking. Meant to be sharing with my group and not with you all the time. But I can't tell them this – they'd throw me out for real. The toilet wouldn't flush and I lifted the lid of the cistern there's a partly drunk bottle of whisky in there. This is the toilet by the front door and I think it was left by someone who had come in for an assessment. I put the bottle in my pocket and went out for a walk down the lane. I went alone (not allowed, but I slipped out without anyone seeing me), hung around in the woods for hours until I felt I was in control enough to go back. Said I was ill and went to bed until the next morning. My room mate (different one now, a young addict) suspects but she's new here and won't say anything.

How easy it was Jules. Just to give in and do it. I'm frightened that I'm going to leave now. I keep talking and talking to everyone but not about what I most need to say. Thank god I can tell you. I tell them here about that car accident I had because it is a distracting dramatic story and I've even still got scars. I was on orange juice all night and John thought I would drive. Of course it wasn't just orange juice. I lost it on a bend and a lorry hit us straight on after we'd come to a standstill. I might have killed him. As it was I got breathalised on the ward because the police were still there when I became conscious. They shouldn't be allowed to do that. I lost my license and had to pretend to John for months that I was afraid of driving. I can't believe how much I managed to deceive him. He was very much in love with me (I was in love with him too) and that's why it was easy. Love isn't the truth it's a crazy thing – I mean that sort of 'in love' love. I'm not doing that again. I think it's like alcoholism and addiction. It's got all the same characteristics: powerlessness, escape from reality (whatever that is), insanity, loss of control. It even makes you sick – at least you feel sick in the stomach (lovesick, the old poets said but no one admits it today).

But this gives me a scary thought. Here I have to give up drink and dope which are insane unreal behaviour. Do I have to give up love too? Here they talk about not being in a relationship for a while when you're recovering from alcohol. They talk about two years. Let me know what you think of this.

Dearest friend Julian I'm in trouble here. I can't tell them about the bottle of whisky. Near the end of my ten weeks I do 'step five' with an outsider who I can tell everything to in complete confidence. It will help. Telling you has helped. Guess what? I understand the concept of powerlessness now. Thank you for listening to me again.

Love from Catrin.

~

Dear Jules

Thanks for your letter. You don't say much (I suppose you're not the writing kind) but I hope you're alright. As for me... well I've got more time today. We do spoken work (these things called shares) and lots of written work. But I'm more manageable (as they say) now and am up to date with my work. It's a warm spell (I hope it's the same for you) and I'm able to sit outside on a garden seat and write this. Being outside of that madhouse calms me. I'm sitting under a big spreading fir tree on an ornate bench looking across to the house which is really something like a mansion. The gardens are landscaped and beautiful but if I spend too much time out here I'm 'isolating' which is 'old behaviour' – I should be with my group. The boss counsellor is the one most against isolating and she's not here today so I may be left in peace. It's a Cedar of Lebanon, I remember now – that's the name of the tree I'm sitting under.

Here we are encouraged/forced to share all our most intimate thoughts, feelings, memories. The people who end up in here have got somewhat out of the habit of doing this – we go in for denial, self-deceit and so on. So it's kleenex-time pretty often and you're brought very close to each other. I'm not going to tell you about the others too much. It's like going through a war together here. Also people you trust lose it and run off. Others leave because they've completed the course. So we're intensely close but it's all very temporary. And these people are the most important ones in changing my life around.

The staff are heroes. But I wonder sometimes. I walked up the corridor to see my counsellor and this posh woman was on the phone at our end phoning home and it's like yes I'm fine and everything is nice here and the people are so kind and I'm having a nice rest. Lies actually – half of us she hates because we tell her stuff she doesn't want to hear and the young guys she treats like they're her children and she's looking after them and so she's got them under control. So, not 'people are kind' and 'I'm having a nice time' – that's not true. OK so I get to the other end of the corridor and there's the big boss (little actually) on the phone with her office door open and everything is fine here and going so well and (wait for it) it's exactly the same tone of voice as at the other end of the corridor. I know that tone of voice – that's the sound of... you know – something beginning with D.

When an office door is shut you know something heavy is going on and you don't knock but just go away and come back later. Well the doors are sometimes shut for hours but we are all in the sittingroom so what's going on? Are they counselling each other? Are they as crazy at their end of the building as we are at ours? I ask the handyman who comes in two days a week and who's approachable. 'The staff are human beings too,' that's all he will say.

I'm slowing down and getting less hyper. I'm changing and most of it is good. You know that whatever the difficulties are there are a million people out there who've been through the same stuff and who can help when I leave here. People like Gareth. Well it's probably more than a million but some aren't much help because they're dangerously screwed up. But some are really really good, so crazy counsellors and bottles hidden in the toilet notwithstanding, I can do this.

I can do this but I might have to do it alone. Julian I can't explain this so well. It seems a cruel thing to say but in a way your kindness supported that craziness of mine. Knowing that you loved me and would always forgive me whatever I did... Do you see?

I want to pay back some of the money I owe to people. You. Gareth. Many others. John. It will take some time. There was one time when I was always moving room. I owed money and would be behind with the rent. Maybe a midnight flit. Maybe hiding when the

181

landlord called. It all seemed part of being a struggling artist. It all
seemed justified by my creativity. A bohemian lifestyle. Very roman-
tic. I think John found it attractive in me but it was bad. No
consideration for others. Once John and I hid in this big kitchen
cupboard because the landlord had keys and had come into the house.
We got caught. John paid my back-rent when he heard that I was
about to be thrown out. I never paid it back like I said I would and
it caused endless rows. My art had to come first I thought. Sometimes
I hoped that John would realise what was going on and help me. But
I hid things from him – how could he have guessed? So he loved me
so much and didn't know me. That's weird. Love is blind.

Look I'm gonna have to go or I'll be in trouble again. I hope this
unseasonable sun shines on your vegetables like it's shining here on my
cedar tree. I'm not sure about you visiting for the time being.

Lots of love

Catrin.

~

Dear Jules

We've got a new resident. We are all frightened of him and no one
admits it. He uses humour. I've never seen this done before. He mimics
people, he takes the piss mercilessly in front of their faces and we all
laugh out loud and it's like what a good time we're having. There's
worse. He has this kind of sexuality. He's not at all handsome but boy
can he flirt. So he's charming and nice and you feel good. Also you
want to be close to that power where it's safe – not on the outside. So
I flirt back and no one challenges it. They're all too intimidated by
him. And even worse I'm actually attracted to him sexually. So he's got
power that way too. Here it's an emotional hothouse and more. There's
the two guys and a young woman too who've come off heroin which,
I'm told, suppresses libido. So no more heroin, guess what. The air full

of lusty feelings. Emotion flowing out of our ears. Laughter. Sexual innuendo and dirty jokes all the time. No sexual liaisons allowed, we're in rehab. And one guy, very charming but nasty under it and he makes me want him. And if I get caught it's twenty minutes to pack.

All the serious talk and sharing have gone and we're laughing and seemingly having a great time but I know the real stuff's not happening now. I'm very scared. We were in the sittingroom today and this Mr Scary was taking the piss and making people laugh. One at a time he was talking about people in the room and putting them down in a nasty way. We all laugh and they have to laugh at themselves too. Sounds OK doesn't it? It's not. To one woman he says he wants to be a godfather to her little boy – presents, kindness etc. He's all charming and nice and we all think what a nice man he is. Then in a quiet voice he says if you die then I get the boy, right? He's mine? Then he's all smiles again but he did that to scare her. Goes quietly to her most vulnerable point. He loves power over people. He gives me very direct sexual looks when no one's around and I feel intimidated and (don't like to admit this) aroused too (well it's been a while). Then he flirts with someone in front of me and I should feel relief but I feel jealousy – wow, such manipulation. I don't know what the counsellors think. Does he charm them? He certainly pretends to do everything he's asked.

I've got to post this. Hope you're alright. Hope I can say more positive things next time.

Love

Catrin.

~

Dear Jules

Good news – Mr Scary is gone. A wonderful gentle stupid old hippy stood up to him, took a chance and told the truth in front of us all. And Mr Scary threw a chair and a counsellor saw and he's out. And we all breathe a sigh of relief. Bad thing: in the garden in the rain, I can't tell anyone else but you so here it is, in the garden I let him... well you know. I had my period a couple of days later so it's not as bad as it might be.

More news. I think I mentioned a woman who I shared a room with when I was first here. She's dead. It's unbelievable (except that it was inevitable) but imagine if you can the shock we all feel here. Drank herself to an early grave. So terrible sadness here for some days. Fear. A lesson. I thought she was going to be alright – she was doing really well and left here on a high point. Two weeks later... I'm afraid it's true.

Can they send you a questionnaire? You will have to write about me honestly. Let them and me know how it was to be in the company of an alcoholic. Please Jules you have to be honest and not too kind. Thank you.

But what about John? I don't want them to send him one and am pretending I have no way of contacting him. He never knew what was going on. I was too clever for him – too much of a cunning addict. Only one thing that he should know one day is that I did love him – that much was always true.

How much I mention that man in these letters after years of carefully blocking out any thoughts or memories. But part of being here is uncovering buried stuff. A big part. I'm sorry if it's hurtful to you. How honest should I be? How honest (even between us) is right? OK here goes:

1) I think of him very often
2) with less anger now but still lots
3) I'll never see him again
4) anyway I have to try to not be in a relationship for a while
5) sometimes I'm writing to you and it's not to you. It's taken me some time to realise it. Sometimes I'm writing to him.

Many many times sorry. Sorry for being honest. Honesty is a relief. But surely there's a time when you go too far and honesty hurts someone (they don't admit that here). I'm learning all this, it seems, from scratch. I need to know how you feel about all of this.

I'm struggling with this concept of higher power. I don't like it *when someone says oh that good thing that's happened that was defi-nitely HP – alright where was HP when the bad things happened? But I need to think of something that will always be with me and always help. Sometimes, outdoors in the garden, I get good feelings that seem deep. Maybe a bird singing. Sunshine. I think of your love of the land and all the nature stuff you tried to give me. Maybe there's some HP in all this. And there's another thing – it's about me choos-ing to always live by the sea. I felt I had an artistic reason. Maybe. But it stood for something else too – something like oblivion. So I think I should live somewhere else when I get out of here. That's my plan at the moment, and in fairness to you I have to say what's on my mind.*

It's all up and down here. You think you are doing well and then the next day it's a cliff edge again. I can't give you a real sense of the intensity of it all in letters. We are all going through this stuff all the time. The truth hurts and it's difficult (even though I'm really deter-mined now) to stay alright and not feel like the ground is giving way beneath you. The staff seem to have their own problems. There's so much going on with other residents. It's all so uncertain and so unreal. But there's one or two people here who make you feel it can be done. Thank god.

And thank you Jules as ever.

Love from Catrin.

~

Dear Julian

Hi. Three in the morning but I feel I have to write.

You've heard me talk about my brother, Tim, but you never met him. Well, he's been to visit. He was in America but now he's back in the UK. You know he's had a wild, wild life. A lot of crack cocaine. Sex with guys as well as women. He had to be completely clean to visit me here – he would no way be allowed in if he smelled of alcohol or seemed stoned. And you know he can do it quite easily. That's strange for me to understand in here surrounded by people who simply have no control over their intake. They – we, I mean – have to stop completely or give in completely. Tim is wild but he's different from me in that respect. It was difficult for us to understand each other's situations but we did understand a bit and it's good because all these things are steps along the road of my recovery.

He's been here to visit twice and today, the second time, I'm left feeling pretty screwed up. So it's three in the morning and I can't sleep because words are going through my head and if I write them down it will help. So – here goes.

Sometimes you have something here called a family conference. A counsellor chairs a meeting between you and one or more of your family or suchlike. The counsellor directs things and tries to bring out the stuff that needs to be said. It takes place, if it's warm enough, in an old stone gazebo in the grounds. Neutral territory. Not so intimidating for the visitor as being in the house. And quiet.

So imagine it if you will: Tim, me, the geordie counsellor I've told you about. The gazebo, quite warm when the sun comes in through the glass doors. Lots of stuff about my childhood – my mother mentally ill, me having to be responsible and so on. Probing questions from the counsellor. Tim very honest and very kind. And we talk about me when I was, to all intents and purposes, a teenage mum (looking after Tim). How that changed me. It's true I never wanted to play that role again. It was too hard and scary and why can't I be a bit selfish and live for me after that?

All this is OK.

Next it's about John. The counsellor asks Tim about John and me. Tim says he didn't think John was such a brilliant guy but he liked him and wanted it to work between us. He wanted John to stay with me, wanted it to be alright and that's why he left that time very suddenly and without explanation. Why did you have to leave? the counsellor asks. I'm relaxed. I know it's because he and John fell out. John was jealous of how close I was to my brother. But I look at Tim and I see... well you know those cartoons where some rabbit or what-

ever has run off the edge of a cliff and they stay up in the air and somehow get back? That's how Tim looks. Panicked.

Tim – (something like this) OK I'll tell you all about it. I guess (looks at me) this is the truth-and-reconciliation-no-more-skeletons-in-the-cupboard moment?

Me – nodding in agreement.

Tim – you know how he was always jealous of you? Like he thought you were screwing around. That always seemed so unfair to me. You weren't – I know you loved him very much. Unfair because he wasn't 100% faithful.

Me – looking shocked. Not in any way guessing what will come next.

Tim – that last night I was at your place and I was playing piano in the pub. John looking across the room towards me all the time. Me flirting. Singing romantic songs, being vain, exhibitionistic etc. And then you're pissed into oblivion. We have to carry you back and John and I sit up late smoking dope. You need to know I didn't start it. And it's a myth that there are no bisexual men – that men are all either gay or straight. Do I really have to say more? Actually I do. We didn't do much but the sex isn't really the point. There were some warm feelings there. Perhaps that's more serious. The feelings John had were maybe transferred from you to me because I'm your brother. I don't know. I didn't make the first move. That's it. You didn't know about this did you?

Me – shocked, not speaking.

Tim – Well, I thought you had a good chance with John and I needed to not be there. And how could I explain? I left in a hurry because I thought it was the best thing for you.

Julian, he said something like that. He didn't totally understand the way it happened and that's maybe how things are sometimes. He said that John was transferring feelings from me to him and the counsellor was very keen on this so maybe it's true.

You know I've been here ten weeks. I've heard some stories. I should be unshockable by now. But Tim is my brother. And I was there in the room for god's sake. It is going to take some time to get my head around this.

Should I tell you this or put the letter in the bin? It's served its purpose – I've gone over the whole thing in my mind. Heard Tim's voice again saying that stuff. Now all sorts of things go through my head. I mean, you spend a lot of time with John, don't you?

So I send this. Write back.

Love Catrin.

~

Dear Julian

Sorry I haven't written for a while. I'm near the end of my stay here and it feels like it's been forever. I came in here and hated everything they said and tried to do to me. Like it was brainwashing or something. Now I accept their ideas of me, my behaviour and how peoples lives work. But we have this way of thinking about things and dealing with things in here that isn't necessarily going to work outside. This place makes you institutionalised and then you leave. Then I will need to go away from people and places that supported/encouraged my drinking. Put myself somewhere where the only people I'm in contact with are clean and in some way understanding of this illness. But even thinking of leaving this place is frightening. OK so I tried to run away three times. Now I don't want to go. But this here is unreal. It's nothing like normal life. I have to carefully create a way of understanding things that seems real and meaningful and workable. I can't say all this to the people here. They want it all simple and if I question and think about stuff I'm criticised for 'intellectualising'. They keep repeating slogans at you – 'it works if you work it', 'one day at a time' and so on. Like second rate religious mantras. The last board you get often says 'give it away to keep it' – meaning help others out of this stuff and you will keep your own sanity. I suggested 'the more I give the more I have'. It's from Shakespeare you know. They hated me for tinkering with their creed. I was only trying to help and they were angry with me for this. Like I'm undermining their faith.

Of course 'the more I give the more I have' is about love and when I told them it was from Romeo and Juliet they went bananas. Like I have to renounce all that stuff. Well I will for a while. I'll find my own strength. (Guess who first said 'the more I...' to me. OK so you don't want to know. Well of all the unrealnesses of my life those times with John were the best beyond anything. When I'm really well maybe those things can happen to me again. But this is not what you want to hear or I need to be thinking about).

Jules it's moving towards warmer days and better weather here. It's good. Daffodils are out and some very delicate cream white flowers I've seen on the edge of the woods. They close and hide in the rain and wind and you think they've been destroyed but then it's warm again and they're opening their petals to the sun. Delicate tenacity. I like that.

How are you? Busy in the sunshine preparing the fields for planting? Sorry I took so little interest in your stuff over the years. Look I'm waffling on and trying to put off some selfish but necessary things I need to say: first I'm not going to see you for some time when I get out of here. There, I've said it. Sorry. And you've been so good to me. Something else and this is selfish in a way but it may perhaps be possible for you. You don't have to do this and I've no right to ask. But there are things in the letters I've written to you that explain a lot about a time in my life that was so good (and sometimes so bad) that I stopped myself from thinking about it afterwards because it hurt too much. It was the best thing. I can't write and explain to him – I can't bear to do it. OK so here goes – this is what I've got to ask you. Will you lend these letters to John to read so that he can understand? I guess you two are pretty close. I don't know how big a thing this is to ask and you can decide not to of course. Do what feels right. Thanks.

And thank you a million times for all sorts of things. I will write again but not so often.

Bye for now,

Love Catrin.

SEVENTEEN

The bay is a long curve of land meeting sea. Notched into the curve are the estuaries where rivers come down out of the hills and flow through wide valleys before losing themselves in the greater expanse of saltwater. The mouth of this estuary is half-closed by a bank of dunes stretching out from the south shore. This is where Julian and I stand at the edge of the water with our two canoes, watching the tide rushing in at our feet. The broad sandbanks in the middle of the estuary, the beaches at its mouth, the mudflats and the saltmarshes, are all gradually disappearing under the incoming seawater. A few hours from now, at high tide, there will be a vast lake of salt-water filling the funnel-shaped space between the hills. It is early morning and the sun is about to rise from behind the hills inland. The light is gentle, the colours of the land and water half-formed. We climb awkwardly into the canoes and push ourselves out into the water.

We paddle first towards the north shore where there is a small town fronted with jetties, piers and a collection of moored boats. The morning air is cold but crossing here we are working hard against the current and are soon warm from our exertions. When we reach the middle of the estuary the expanse of water seems very great and our progress is slow. We can see out past the dunes to where the sea builds large waves on the submerged sand-banks. Close to the north shore we rest, allowing ourselves to be swept along by the tide. The land drifts past: oak woods on the steeper slopes, pastures with sheep and cattle, saltmarshes along the edge of the shore disappearing under the encroaching seawater. Then we are passing close to a rock promontory. The water flows fast here, piling up into little steep waves as it passes over the rocks below the surface. A broad eddy sweeps us around, out of control for a moment until we are pushed out into calmer water.

As the morning progresses we float further away from the sea and into the broad space between the hills, sometimes using the paddles to push ourselves along, sometimes just drifting with the tide. I have pulled away from Julian and am on my own. I am a good way out from the shore and travelling through water so still that it forms a perfect mirror to the sky above. The sun has risen and brightened, low-lit white clouds float in the blue above and below me. I find my eyes fixed on the piece of sky that is the water in front of the boat. I move through this sky and it shimmers and breaks as the point of the canoe touches it. And ahead there is always more pure undisturbed space for me to travel into. Then a small breeze comes out of a gap in the hills, ruffles the water and breaks the reflection. I drift, letting the boat turn, a panorama of sunlit landscape circling me. Julian gradually catches up. As he gets closer he opens his mouth to speak but says nothing. He raises his eyebrows as if asking a question. He smiles. His boat drifts into mine and we both spin slowly in the current, joined together for a while, seeing the same changing scenes as we turn.

Later, further inland, we are paddling close to a steep grassy slope that faces the sun. The light is reflected off the water and makes a constantly changing pattern of ripples on the grass. Travelling through this superimposed water and across the grass is the perfect shadow of a small boat with a man in it. He stops moving when I stop. Close by is another shadow boat with a man waving. It drifts through the grazing cattle. I wave back.

THE AUTHOR

Richard Collins has been a farm labourer, gardener and estate worker. He lives with his family in west Wales and teaches at the Institute of Rural Sciences in Llanbadarn. *The Land as Viewed from the Sea* is his first novel.